PENGUIN BOOKS

THE CORPSE EXHIBITION

HASSAN BLASIM was born in Baghdad in 1973 and studied at the Baghdad Academy of Cinematic Arts. A critic of Saddam Hussein's regime, he was persecuted and in 1998 fled Baghdad to Iraqi Kurdistan, where he made films and taught filmmaking under the pseudonym Ouazad Osman. In 2004, a year into the war, he fled to Finland, where he now lives. A filmmaker, poet, and fiction writer, he has published in various magazines and anthologies and is a coeditor of the Arabic literary website www.iraqstory.com. His fiction has twice won the English PEN Writers in Translation award and has been translated into Finnish, Polish, Spanish, and Italian. In 2012 a heavily edited version of his stories was finally published in Arabic and was immediately banned in Jordan.

JONATHAN WRIGHT (translator) studied Arabic at Oxford University and has spent much of the past three decades in the Arab world, mostly as a journalist with Reuters.

THE CORPSE EXHIBITION

AND OTHER STORIES OF IRAQ

HASSAN BLASIM

Translated from the Arabic by
Jonathan Wright

PENGUIN BOOKS

PENGUIN BOOKS
Published by the Penguin Group
Penguin Group (USA) LLC
375 Hudson Street
New York, New York 10014

USA | Canada | UK | Ireland | Australia | New Zealand | India | South Africa | China
penguin.com
A Penguin Random House Company

First published in Penguin Books 2014

The Madman of Freedom Square
Copyright © 2009 by Hassan Blasim
Translation copyright © 2009 by Jonathan Wright
Collection copyright © 2009 by Comma Press

The Iraqi Christ
Copyright © 2013 by Hassan Blasim
Translation copyright © 2013 by Jonathan Wright
Collection copyright © 2013 by Comma Press

The stories in *The Corpse Exhibition* appeared in Hassan Blasim's *The Madman of
Freedom Square* and *The Iraqi Christ*, both published in Great Britain by Comma
Press. The following selections appeared in *The Madman of Freedom Square*:
"The Corpse Exhibition," "An Army Newspaper," "The Madman of Freedom Square,"
"The Composer," "The Reality and the Record," "That Inauspicious Smile," and
"The Nightmares of Carlos Fuentes." The following stories were published in
The Iraqi Christ: "The Killers and the Compass," "The Green Zone Rabbit,"
"Crosswords," "The Hole," "The Iraqi Christ," "A Thousand and One Knives," and
"The Song of the Goats." "The Reality and the Record" was first published in *Madinah:
City Stories from the Middle East*, edited by Joumana Haddad (Comma Press, 2008).
"The Green Zone Rabbit" was first published by Words Without Borders.

Excerpt from *The Forgotten Language: An Introduction to the Understanding of
Dreams, Fairy Tales and Myths* by Erich Fromm (New York: Rinehart & Co., Inc., 1951).

ISBN 978-0-14-312326-2

Printed in the United States of America
3   5   7   9   10   8   6   4

Set in Mercury Text G1
Designed by Sabrina Bowers

Contents

THE CORPSE EXHIBITION

The Corpse Exhibition

BEFORE TAKING OUT HIS KNIFE HE SAID, "AFTER studying the client's file you must submit a brief note on how you propose to kill your first client and how you will display his body in the city. But that doesn't mean that what you propose in your note will be approved. One of our specialists will review the proposed method and either approve it or propose a different method. This system applies to professionals in all phases of their work—even after the training phase has ended and you have taken the test. In all phases you will receive your salary in full. I don't want to go into all the details now. I'll brief you on things gradually. After you receive the client's file you cannot ask questions as you could before. You have to submit your questions in writing. All your questions, proposals, and written submissions will be documented in your personal file. You absolutely may not write to me about work matters by e-mail or call me on the phone. You will write your questions on a special form that I will provide you with later. The important thing is that you now devote your time to studying the client's file carefully and patiently.

"I want to reassure you that we won't stop dealing with you even if you fail in your first assignment. If you fail you'll be transferred to work in another department at the same salary. But I must remind you once again: Giving up the job after you receive your first salary payment would be unacceptable and would not succeed. There are strict conditions for that, and if the management agrees to sever relations with you, you would have to undergo many tests, which could last a long time. In the archives we have files we preserve about volunteers and other agents who decided to terminate their contracts on their own initiative. If you're thinking of doing that, we'll show you some examples of the experiences of others. I'm confident you'll be able to persevere with the work and enjoy it. You'll see how your whole life will change.

"This is your first present; don't open it now. It's your pay in full. As for the documentaries about the lives of predatory animals, you can buy them and we'll cover the expenses later. Pay particular attention to the images of the victims' bones.

"Always remember, dear friend, that we are not terrorists whose aim is to bring down as many victims as possible in order to intimidate others, nor even crazy killers working for the sake of money. We have nothing to do with the fanatical Islamist groups or the intelligence agency of some nefarious government or any of that kind of nonsense.

"I know you now have some questions that are nagging you, but you will gradually discover that the world is built to have more than one level, and it's unrealistic for everyone to reach all the levels and all the basements with ease. Don't forget the senior positions that await you in the hierarchy of the institution if you have an imagination that is fresh, fierce, and striking.

"Every body you finish off is a work of art waiting for you to add the final touch, so that you can shine like a precious jewel amid the wreckage of this country. To display a corpse for others to see is the ultimate in the creativity we are seeking and that we are trying to study and benefit from. Personally I can't stand the agents who are unimaginative. We have, for example, an agent whose code name is Satan's Knife, that I wish those in charge would get rid of as soon as possible. This guy thinks that cutting off the client's limbs and hanging them from the electrical wires in the slum neighborhoods is the height of creativity and inventiveness. He's just a conceited fool. I hate his classical methods, although he talks about a new classicism. All this lightweight does is paint the client's body parts and hang them from invisible threads, the heart in dark blue, the intestines green, the liver and testicles yellow. He does this without understanding the poetry of simplicity.

"When I tell you some of the details I see that puzzled look in your eyes. Calm down, breathe deep, listen to the rhythm of your secret spirit calmly and patiently. Let me explain some points to you more clearly to dispel some of the misapprehensions you may have. Let me waste some time with you. What I tell you may be just personal impressions, and another member of the group may have a quite different opinion.

"I like concision, simplicity, and the striking image. Take Agent Deaf, for example. He's calm, and he has a smart, lucid eye, and my favorite work of his was that woman who was breast-feeding. One rainy winter's morning a crowd of passersby and drivers stopped to look at that woman. She was naked and fat, and her child, also naked, was suckling at her left breast. He put the woman under a dead palm tree in the central reservation of a busy street. There was no trace of a wound or a bullet on the woman's body or on the baby's. She and her baby looked as alive as a brook of pure water. That's a genius we lack in this century. You should have seen the woman's enormous tits and how thin the baby was, like a pile of bones painted the color of bright white baby skin. No one could work out how the mother and her child were killed. Most people speculated that he used some mysterious poison that has not yet been classified. But you should read in the archives in our library the brief, poetic report that Deaf wrote on this extraordinary work of art. He now holds an important position in the group. He deserves much more than that.

"You must understand properly that this country presents one of the century's rare opportunities. Our work may not last long. As soon as the situation stabilizes we'll have to move on to another country. Don't worry, there are many candidates. Listen, in the past we offered new students like you classical lessons, but now things are much changed. We've started to rely on the democracy and spontaneity of the imagination, and not on instruction. I studied a long time and read many boring books justifying what we do before I was able to work professionally. We used to read studies that spoke about peace, studies written with really disgusting eloquence. There were many naive and unnecessary analogies to justify everything. One of them was about how all the medicines at the pharmacy, even plain old toothpaste, were produced after laboratory tests on rats and other animals, so it would not be possible to bring about peace on this earth without sacrificing laboratory humans as well. Old lessons like these were boring and frustrating. Your generation is very lucky in this age of golden opportunities. A film actress licking an ice cream might give rise to dozens of photographs and news reports that reach the most remote village ravished by famine in this world, this grindstone of screaming and dancing. This at least achieves what I call 'the justice of discovering the insignificance and equivocal essence of the world.' How much more so a corpse displayed creatively in the city center!

"Perhaps I've told you too much, but let me tell you frankly that I'm worried about you, because you're either an idiot or a genius, and agents like that excite my curiosity. If you're a genius, that would be gratifying. I still believe in genius, although most members of the group talk about experience and practice. And if you're an idiot, let me tell you before I go a short and useful story about one idiot who naively tried to mess with us. I didn't even like his nickname—'the Nail.' After the committee had approved the way the Nail proposed to kill his client and display his body in a large restaurant, we waited for results. But this guy was very slow about finishing off his work. I met him several times and asked him what was causing the delay. He would say that he didn't want to repeat the methods of his predecessors and was thinking of bringing about a creative quantum leap in our work. But the truth was different. The Nail was a coward who had been infected with banal humanitarian feelings and, like any sick man, had started to question the benefit of killing others and to wonder whether there was some creator monitoring all our deeds, and that was the beginning of the abyss. Because every child born in this world is simply a possibility, either to be good or evil, according to the classification set by schools of religious education in this stupid world. But it's a completely different matter for us. Every child that's born is just an extra burden on the ship that's about to sink. Anyway, let me tell you what happened to the Nail. He had a relative who worked as a guard in the hospital in the city center, and the Nail was thinking of slipping into the hospital mortuary and choosing a corpse instead of making a corpse himself. It was easy to carry that off after he'd given his relative half the pay he'd received from the group. The mortuary was full of corpses from those stupid acts of terrorism, corpses ripped apart by car bombs, others that had their heads cut off in sectarian feuds, bloated bodies from the riverbed, and many other stupid ones that had been finished off in random murders that had nothing to do with art. The Nail slipped into the mortuary that night and started looking for the right corpse to display to the public. The Nail was looking for the children's corpses, because in his first report he had proposed an idea that involved killing a five-year-old child.

"In the mortuary there were specimens of the corpses of schoolchildren who had been mutilated by car bombs or incinerated in some street market or broken into pieces after planes bombed houses. Finally the Nail chose a child who had been beheaded along with the rest of his family for sectarian reasons. The body was clean, and the cut at the neck was as neat as a piece of torn paper. The Nail thought of exhibiting this body in a restaurant and putting the eyes of the other family members on the table, served in bowls of blood, like a soup. Maybe it was a beautiful idea, but before all else his work would have been a cheat and a betrayal. If he had beheaded the child himself it would have been an authentic work of art, but to steal it from the mortuary and act in this despicable manner would be a disgrace and cowardice at the same time. But he did not understand that the world today is linked together by more than a tunnel and a corridor.

"It was the mortician who caught the Nail before he was able to deceive the poor public. The mortician was in his early sixties, an enormous man. His work in the mortuary had flourished after the increase in the number of mutilated bodies in the country. People sought him out to patch together the bodies of their children and other relatives who were torn apart in explosions and random killings. They would pay handsomely to have him restore their children to the appearance by which they originally knew them. The mortician was truly a great artist. He worked with patience and with great love. That night he guided the Nail into a side room in the mortuary and locked the door on him. He injected him with some drug that paralyzed him without making him unconscious. He laid him out on the mortuary table, strapped his hands and legs down, and gagged his mouth. He was humming a pretty children's song in his strange woman's voice as he prepared his worktable. It was a song about a child fishing for a frog in a small puddle of blood, and every now and then he would stroke the Nail's hair tenderly and whisper in his ear, 'Ooh, my dear, ooh, my friend, there is something stranger than death—to look at the world, which is looking at you, but without any gesture or understanding or even purpose, as though you and the world are united in blindness, like silence and loneliness. And there is something a little stranger than death: a man and a woman playing in bed, and then you come, just you, you who always miswrite the story of your life.'

"The mortician finished his work in the early morning.

"In front of the gate of the Ministry of Justice there was a platform like the platforms on which the city's statues stand, but made of a pulp of flesh and bones. On top of the platform stood a pillar of bronze, and from the pillar hung the Nail's skin, complete and detached from his flesh with great skill, waving like a flag of victory. In the front part of the platform you could clearly see the Nail's right eye, set in the pulp of his flesh. It had a look rather like the insipid look your eyes have now. Do you know who the mortician was? He's the man in charge of the most important department in the institution. He's the man in charge of the truth and creativity department."

Then he thrust the knife into my stomach and said, "You're shaking."

The Killers and the Compass

ABU HADID KNOCKED BACK WHAT REMAINED OF THE bottle of arak.* He put his face close to mine and, with the calm of someone high on hashish, gave me this advice: "Listen, Mahdi. I've seen all kinds of problems in my life, and I know that one day I'll run out of luck. You're six-teen, and today I'm going to teach you how to be a lion. In this world you need to be street-smart. Whether you die today or in thirty years, it doesn't make any difference. It's today that matters and whether you can see the fear in people's eyes. People who are frightened will give you everything. If someone tells you, 'God forbids it' or 'That's wrong,' for example, give him a kick up the ass, because that god's full of shit. That's their god, not your god. *You* are your own god, and this is your day. There's no god without followers or crybabies willing to die of hunger or suffer in his name. You have to learn how to make your-self God in this world, so that people lick your ass while you shit down their throats. Don't open your mouth today,

---

* Arak: a traditional anise-flavored distilled spirit.

not a word. You come with me, dumb as a lamb. Under-stand, dickhead?"

He thumped the arak bottle against the wall and aimed a friendly punch hard into my nose.

We walked through the darkness of the muddy lanes. The wretched houses were catching their breath after re-ceiving a whipping from the storm. Inside them the peo-ple were sleeping and dreaming. Everything was soaked and knocked out of place. The wind that had toyed with the labyrinth of lanes all evening picked up strength, then finally left with a bitter chill hanging over the place— this sodden neighborhood where I would live and die. Many times I imagined the neighborhood as if it were some offspring of my mother's. It smelled that way and was just as miserable. I don't recall ever seeing my mother as a human being. She would always be weeping and wail-ing in the corner of the kitchen like a dog tied up to be tor-mented. My father would assail her with a hail of insults, and when her endurance broke, she would whine aloud, "Why, good Lord? Why? Take me and save me."

Only then would my father stand up, take the cord out of his headdress, and whip her nonstop for half an hour, spitting at her throughout.

My nose was bleeding profusely. I was holding my head back as I tried to keep pace with Abu Hadid. The smell of spiced fish wafted from the window of Majid the traffic policeman's house. He must have been blind drunk to be frying fish in the middle of the night. We turned down a narrow, winding lane. Abu Hadid picked up a stone and threw it toward two cats that were fighting on top of a pile of rubbish. They jumped through the window of Abu

Rihab's abandoned house. The rubbish almost reached the roof of the place. The government had executed Abu Rihab and confiscated his house. They say his family went back to the country where their clan lived. Abu Rihab had been in contact with the banned Daawa party. After a year of torture and interrogation in the vaults of the security services, he was branded a traitor and shot. It was impossible to forget the physical presence of his beautiful daughter, Rihab. She was a carbon copy of Jennifer Lopez in *U Turn*. I'd seen the film at the home of Abbas, the poet who lived next door. He had films that wouldn't be shown on state television for a hundred years. Most of the young men in the neighborhood had tried to court Rihab with love letters, but she was an idiot who understood nothing but washing the courtyard and pouring water over the hands of her Daawa party father before he prayed.

Abu Hadid, my giant brother, stopped in front of the door to Umm Hanan's house. She was the widow of Allawi Shukr, and people in the neighborhood made fun of her morals by calling her Hanan Aleena, which means something like "easy favors." We went inside and sat on a wooden bench with an uncomfortable back. Umm Hanan asked one of her daughters to wash my face and take care of me. The girl blocked my nose with cotton wool. Umm Hanan had three beautiful daughters, all alike as nurses in uniform. My brother slept with Umm Hanan. Then he fucked her youngest daughter twice. After that he told Umm Hanan to fuck me. I was surprised he didn't ask that of the girl who was my age. Then Abu Hadid took some money and three packs of cigarettes from Umm Hanan, and gave me one of the packs.

We set off again, walking along the muddy lanes. Abu Hadid slowed down, then retraced his steps and stopped at the door of Abu Mohammed, the car mechanic. He knocked on the door with his foot. The man came out in his white dishdasha with his paunch sticking out. His eyes popped out of his head when Abu Hadid greeted him. Me and the other kids used to call him "the gerbil who swallowed the watermelon." He used to give me and the gang pills in return for puncturing the tires of cars in the neighborhood, so that his business would flourish. We would bargain with him over how many pills for how many tires. My brother ordered me to take off my bloodied shirt and told the mechanic to fetch me a clean one. The gerbil obeyed at once and came back with a blue shirt that smelled of soap. It was the shirt his son, a student at medical college, had just been wearing. I was surprised that the size fit me exactly. My brother leaned over and whispered a few words in the mechanic's ear, and the mechanic's face turned even darker than usual.

We crossed the main street toward the other neighborhood. All along the way I was wondering what Abu Hadid had whispered in the gerbil's ear. Abu Hadid coughed loudly, and his chest wheezed like my uncle's old tractor. He didn't say a single word on the way. He lit two cigarettes at the same time and offered one to me. It was after midnight. I don't know anyone who lives in this neighborhood, other than an obnoxious boy who was at school with us. He once punched me, and I never did manage to stick a finger up his ass in return. When he found out I was Abu Hadid's brother, his father came to school and asked me to beat up his son.

People were scared senseless of my brother's brutality. His reputation for ruthless delinquency spread throughout the city. He would baffle the police and other security agencies for many years—until, that is, the day he was executed in public. Even his enemies mourned him when the inevitable happened. Occasionally in life he had defended people—against the cruelty of the ruling party, for example. Abu Hadid didn't distinguish between good and evil. He had his own private demons. Once he threw a hand grenade at the party office when "the comrades" executed someone who had evaded military conscription. Another time he mutilated the face of some wretched vegetable seller, simply because he was drunk and he felt like it. Abu Hadid would go on the rampage like that for eight years, until Johnny the barber gave him away. The night it happened Abu Hadid was fucking Johnny's pretty brown daughter on the roof of the house. The police surrounded him and shot him in the leg. They executed him a week later. My mother and my seven sisters would beat their breasts for a whole year, but my father was relieved to be rid of the antics of his wayward son.

Abu Hadid knocked on a rusty door that still had a few spots of green paint, shaped like frogs, on it. We were received by a man in his forties with a thick mustache that covered his teeth when he spoke. We sat down in the guest room in front of the television. I gathered that the man lived alone. He went into the kitchen and came back with a bottle of arak. He opened it and poured a glass. My brother told him to pour one for me too. We sat in silence, and the man and I watched a soccer match between two local teams, while my brother stared into a small fish tank.

"Do you think the fish are happy in the tank?" my brother asked, calm and serious.

"As long as they eat and drink and swim, they're fine," the man replied, without looking away from the television screen.

"Do fish drink water?"

"Sure they drink; of course."

"How can fish drink salt water?"

"Sure they have a way. How could they be in water and not drink?"

"If they're in water, perhaps they don't need to drink."

"Why don't you ask the fish in the tank?"

Before the bald man could turn to look at him, my brother had jumped on top of him like a hungry tiger. He threw him to the ground, squatted on his chest, and pinned his arms down under his knees. In a flash he took a small knife out of his pocket, put it close to the man's eye, and started shouting hysterically in his face, "Answer, you cocksucker! How can fish drink salt water? Answer, you son of a bitch! Answer! Do fish drink water or don't they? Answer, shit-for-brains!"

Abu Hadid stuck a cucumber up the man's ass and we left the house. I never would understand what the man had to do with my brother. We headed toward the parking lot. A thin young man, a year younger than my brother, was leaning against a red Chevrolet Malibu dating from the seventies. He embraced my brother warmly, and I felt that Abu Hadid and he were genuine friends. We set off in the car, smoking and listening to a popular song about lovers parting. We took the highway toward the outskirts of the city. Abu Hadid turned off the tape player, lay back in his seat, and said, "Murad, tell my brother the story about the Pakistani kid."

"Sure, no problem," replied Murad Harba.

"Listen, Mahdi. Some years back I took the plunge and escaped to Iran. I was thinking of going from there into Turkey and putting this fucked-up country behind me. I lived in a filthy house in the north of Iran, with people coming from Pakistan, Afghanistan, and Iraq and everywhere on God's pimping earth. We waited for them to hand us over to the Iranian trafficker who was going to take us across the mountainous border. That's where I met the Pakistani kid. He was about your age, nice guy, young and very handsome. He spoke little Arabic, but he had memorized the Quran. He was always scared. And he had a strange object in his possession: a compass. He would hold it in the palm of his hand like a butterfly and stare at it. Then he would hide it in a special pouch that hung around his neck like a golden pendant. He hanged himself in the bathroom the day before Iranian security raided the house. They shoved us in jail and beat us up plenty. When they'd finished humiliating us, we got our breath back and started to get to know the other prisoners. One of the people we chatted with was a young Iraqi who'd been jailed for selling hashish. He was born in Iran. The government had deported his family from Baghdad after the war broke out on the grounds that he had Iranian nationality. I told him about the Pakistani kid who had hanged himself. The man was really upset about the poor boy, said he had met him before, that he was a good kid, and that he knew the whole story of the compass.

"In 1989 in the Pakistani city of Peshawar, Sheikh

Abdullah Azzam, the spiritual father of the jihad in Afghanistan, was in a car on his way to pray in a mosque frequented by the Afghan Arabs—the Arabs who went to fight in Afghanistan. The car was blown up as it crossed a bridge over a storm drain. His two sons were with him and were torn to pieces. According to the muezzin* of the mosque, who rushed to the scene of the explosion as soon as it happened, Azzam's body was seemingly untouched. Not a single scratch. There was just a thin line of blood running from the corner of the dead sheikh's mouth. It was a dreadful disaster—al Qaeda was accused of assassinating the sheikh who had stood up to the might of the Soviet Union, perhaps to give them greater impunity as an organization.

"Before many others had gathered, Malik the muezzin spotted the compass close to the wreckage of the car. When he wiped the blood off it, he felt a shiver run up his spine. It was an army compass with the words *Allah* and *Muhammad* engraved on it. It was clear to the muezzin that it was the sheikh's holy compass, blessed by God and a conduit for his miracles. Many of the mujahideen claimed the compass turned blood-red when God intended good or evil for the person carrying it. Azzam had never parted with it throughout his life in jihad. Malik hid it at home for ten years. He took it out every night, polished it, and looked at it, as he shed tears of sorrow at the death of the mujahideen's sheikh.

"The muezzin placed the compass gently into the hand of his son Waheed, like someone setting down a

---

* Muezzin: the person who calls Muslims to prayer.

precious jewel onto a piece of cloth. Waheed had decided to smuggle his way into England. He might strike lucky there, help his family, and study to become a doctor. The muezzin told his son Waheed the secret of the compass and advised him to guard it with his life. With firm faith, he told him the compass would help him on his journey and throughout his life, and that it was the most precious thing a father could offer his son. Waheed was unaware of the compass's powers and significance, and didn't know much about those holy and special moments when the compass turned red to warn of good or evil, but his faith in his father made him treasure it. The compass then became inseparable from his person.

Waheed reached Iran and lived in dilapidated houses run by traffickers. He had to work six months to save enough money to make the crossing to Turkey. One day he went out with six young Afghans to work on a building site. A rich Iranian man picked them up in a small truck and drove them to the outskirts of the town, where he was building an enormous house in the middle of his farm. They were working for a pittance. The man dropped them off at his farm and asked them to clear away the bricks, plaster, sacks, and wood left over from the building work. The deal was that the owner would come back late that evening and take them back to town. He gave them half their wages in advance and advised them to finish the work properly. Waheed and the Afghans worked slowly and lazily all day long. When the sun set they all prayed and then sat down to relax in one of the large rooms. They poured some juice, rolled cigarettes, and started to chat about trafficking routes to Europe. Every now and then

the young Afghans would give Waheed sly looks of contempt. The owner was late. The Afghans decided to pass
the time by playing a betting game, which was really a
malicious trick. There was a group of barrels filled with
water, next to some bags full of plaster. They told Waheed
the game was that they would mix the plaster with water
in a barrel and everyone in the group would put his hands
in the mixture up to his elbow, and whoever managed to
keep them in the longest would win a sum of money. They
suggested Waheed go first. Full of good cheer and inno-
cence, Waheed stood up and went through the motions,
burying his arms in the plaster mixture. Within a few
minutes the plaster set hard and Waheed's arms were
trapped in the barrel. The Afghans pulled down Waheed's
trousers and raped him one by one."

Between us we smoked nine cigarettes while listening
to the story about the Pakistani. Murad Harba spat out
his tale in one burst, then drank from the bottle of water
next to him, cursing God. Abu Hadid took his pistol out of
his belt and started to load it with bullets. The story about
the Pakistani had no effect on me. I was entranced by the
company of my brother Abu Hadid and by the chance to
enter his various worlds. We turned off into an extensive
park with bare trees like soldiers turned to stone. Murad
switched off the engine. My heart was starting to pound,
and I was curious to find out what they would do in the
darkness of the cold park. Obviously we hadn't come all
this way to listen to the story about the Pakistani. We got
out of the car. Abu Hadid looked around while Murad
Harba opened the trunk of the car and took out a pick and
shovel. Abu Hadid ordered me to help Murad dig. My

blood began to race with excitement and fear. Abu Hadid, with his strong muscles, helped with the digging. We began to sweat. The ground was tough. The tangled roots of a tree and a large stone hampered our work. Before we'd had time to catch our breath, Murad and Abu Hadid headed back to the trunk of the car, while I stood close to the hole, bewildered like a deaf man at a wedding party. They took a man, bound and gagged, out of the trunk and dragged him along the ground to the hole. My brother told me to come close and look into the man's eyes. The look of fear I saw is stamped in my memory as though with a branding iron. Abu Hadid kicked him in the back, and the man slumped into the hole. We shoveled soil on top of him and leveled the ground well.

Abu Hadid gave my hair a sharp tug and whispered in my ear:

"Now you're God."

The Green Zone Rabbit

BEFORE THE EGG APPEARED, I WOULD READ A BOOK about law or religion every night before going to sleep. Like my rabbit, I would be most active in the hours around dawn and sunset. Salsal, on the other hand, would stay up late at night and wake up at midday. And before he even got out of bed he would open his laptop and log on to Facebook to check the latest comments on the previous night's discussion, then eventually go and have a bath. After that he would go into the kitchen, turn on the radio, and listen to the news while he fried an egg and made some coffee. He would carry his breakfast into the garden and sit at the table under the umbrella, eating and drinking and smoking as he watched me.

"Good morning, Hajjar. What news of the flowers?"

"It's been a hot year, so they won't grow strong," I told him as I pruned the rosebushes.

Salsal lit another cigarette and gave my rabbit an ironic smile. I never understood why he was annoyed by the rabbit. The old woman Umm Dala had brought it. She said she had found it in the park. We decided to keep it while Umm Dala looked for its owner. The rabbit had been with us for a month, and I had already spent two months with Salsal in this fancy villa in the north of the Green Zone. The villa was detached, surrounded by a high wall with a gate fitted with a sophisticated electronic security system. We didn't know when zero hour would come. Salsal was a professional, whereas they called me "duckling" because this was my first operation.

Mr. Salman would visit us once a week to check how we were and reassure us about things. Mr. Salman would bring some bottles of booze and some hashish. He would always tell us a silly joke about politics and remind us how secret and important the operation was. This Salman was in league with Salsal and didn't reveal many secrets to me. Both of them made much of my weakness and lack of experience. I didn't pay them much attention. I was sunk in the bitterness of my life, and I wanted the world to be destroyed in one fell swoop.

Umm Dala would come two days a week. She would bring us cigarettes and clean the house. On one occasion Salsal harassed her. He touched her bottom while she was cooking dolma. She hit him on the nose with her spoon and made it bleed. Salsal laid off her and didn't speak to her after that. She was an energetic woman in her fifties with nine children. She claimed she hated men, saying they were despicable, selfish pricks. Her husband had worked for the national electric company, but he fell from the top of a lamppost and died. He was a drunkard and she used to call him the arak gerbil.

I built the rabbit a hutch in the corner of the garden and took good care of him. I know rabbits are sensitive creatures and need to be kept clean and well fed. I read about that when I was in high school. I developed a passion for reading when I was thirteen. In the beginning I read classical Arabic poetry and lots of stories translated from Russian. But I soon grew bored. Our neighbor worked in the Ministry of Agriculture, and one day I was playing with his son Salam on the roof of their house, when we came across a large wooden trunk up there with assorted junk piled up on top of it. Salam shared a secret with me. The trunk was crammed with books about crops and irrigation methods and countless encyclopedias about plants and insects. Under the books there were lots of sex magazines with pictures of Turkish actresses. Salam gave me a magazine, but I also took a book about the various types of palm trees that grow in the country. I didn't need Salam after that. I would sneak from our house to the roof of theirs to visit the library in the trunk. I would take one book and one magazine and put back the ones I had borrowed. After that I fell in love with books about animals and plants and would hunt down every new book that reached the bookshops, until I was forced to join the army.

The pleasure I found in reading books was disconcerting, however. I felt anxious about every new piece of information. I would latch onto one particular detail and start looking for references and other versions of it in other writings. I remembered, for example, that for quite some time I tracked down the subject of kissing. I read and read and felt dizzy with the subject, as if I had eaten some psychotropic fruit. Experiments have shown that chimpanzees resort to kissing as a way to reduce tension, fatigue, and fear among the group. It's been proven that female chimpanzees, when they feel that strangers have entered their territory, hurry to their mates, hug them, and start kissing them. And after long research, I came across another kiss, a long tropical kiss. A kiss by a type of tropical fish that kiss each other for half an hour or more without any kind of break. My memory of those years of darkness under sanctions is of devouring books. The electricity would go off for up to twenty hours a day, especially after that series of U.S. air strikes on the presidential palaces. I would snuggle into bed at midnight, and by the light of a candle I would stumble upon another species of kiss: by insects called Reduvius, though they don't actually kiss each other. These only like the mouths of sleeping humans. They crawl across the face till they reach the corner of the mouth, where they settle down and start kissing. When they kiss they secrete poison in microscopic drops, and if the person sleeping is in good health and sleeping normally, he'll wake up with a poisonous kiss on his mouth the size of four large raindrops put together.

I ran away from military service. I couldn't endure the system of humiliation there. At night I worked in a bakery. I had to support my mother and my five brothers. I lost the urge to read. For me the world became like an incomprehensible mythical animal. A year after I ran away, the regime was overthrown and I was free of my fear of punishment for my earlier desertion. The new government abolished conscription. When the cycle of violence and the sectarian decapitations began, I planned to escape the country and go to Europe, but then they massacred two of my remaining brothers. They were coming back from work in a local factory that made women's shoes. The taxi driver handed them over at a fake checkpoint. The Allahu

Akbar militias took them away to an undisclosed location. They drilled lots of holes in their bodies with an electric drill and then cut off their heads. We found their bodies in a garbage dump on the edge of the city.

I was completely devastated and I left home. I couldn't bear to see the horror on the faces of my mother and brothers. I felt lost and no longer knew what I still wanted from this life. I took a room in a dirty hotel until my uncle came to visit me and suggested I work with his sect. To exact revenge.

The summer days were long and tedious. It's true that the villa was comfortable, with a swimming pool and a sauna. But to me it seemed like a palatial mirage. Salsal took a room on the second floor, while I was content with a cover and a pillow on the sofa in the middle of the large sitting room where the bookcase stood. I wanted to keep an eye on the garden and the outer gate of the villa, in case anything unexpected happened. I was stunned by the size of the bookcase in the sitting room. It had many volumes on religion and on local and international law. Along the shelves, animals made of teak had been arranged in shapes and poses reminiscent of African totems. The animals also separated the religious books from the law books. As soon as it fell dark, I would grab a bite to eat and go and surrender myself to the sofa, reminisce a little about the events of my life, then take out a book and read distractedly. The world in my head was like a spiderweb that made a faint hum, the hum of a life about to expire, of breaths held. Delicate, horrible wings flapping for the last time.

I found the egg three days before Mr. Salman's last visit. One day I woke up at dawn, as usual. I fetched some clean water and food and went to inspect my friend the rabbit. I opened his hutch and he hopped out into the garden. There was an egg in the hutch. I picked it up and examined it, trying to understand the absurdity of it. It was too small to be a chicken's egg. I was anxious, so I went straight to Salsal's room. I woke him up and told him about it. Salsal took hold of the egg and stared at it for a while, then laughed sneeringly.

"Hajjar, you'd better not be pulling my leg," he said, pointing his finger toward my eye.

"What do you mean? It wasn't me who laid the egg!" I said firmly.

Salsal rubbed his eyes, then suddenly jumped out of bed like a madman, firing curses at me. We headed to the villa gate and checked the security system. We inspected the walls and searched the garden and all the rooms. There were no signs of anything unusual. But an egg in a rabbit hutch! Our only option was to think that someone was playing tricks on us, sneaking into the villa and putting the egg next to the rabbit.

"Perhaps it's a silly stunt by that whore Umm Dala. Damn you and your rabbit," said Salsal, but then he went quiet.

Both of us knew that Umm Dala was sick and hadn't come to visit us for the past week. We were doubly afraid because we didn't have any guns in the house. We weren't allowed to have guns until the day of the mission. They were worried about random searches because the Green Zone was a government area and most of the politicians lived there. We were living in the villa on the pretense that we were bodyguards to a member of Parliament.

Salsal threw a fit and asked me to slaughter the rabbit, but I refused and told him the rabbit had nothing to do with what had happened.

"Wasn't it your bloody rabbit that laid the egg?" he said angrily as he went up to his room.

I made some coffee and sat in the garden, watching the rabbit, which was eating its own droppings. They say the droppings contain vitamin B produced by tiny organisms in its intestines. After a while Salsal came back carrying his laptop. He was mumbling to himself and cursing Mr. Salman from time to time. He looked at his Facebook page and said we had to be on alert 24-7. He asked me to spend the night in his room on the second floor because it was good for monitoring the gate and the walls of the villa.

We turned off all the lights, sat in Salsal's room, and every now and then took turns making a tour of inspection around the villa.

Two nights passed without anything suspicious. The villa was quiet, sunk in silence and calm. While I was staying in Salsal's room I learned he was registered with Facebook under the pseudonym War and Peace and had posted a charcoal drawing of Tolstoy as his profile picture. He had more than a thousand Facebook friends, most of them writers, journalists, and intellectuals. He would discuss their ideas and pose as an intelligent admirer of other Facebook people. He expressed his opinions and his analysis of the violence in the country with modesty and wisdom. He even tried it with me, rambling on about the character of the Deputy Minister of Culture. He told me how cultured and humane and uniquely intelligent he was. At the time I wasn't interested in talking about the deputy minister. I told him that people who work in our line of business ought to keep their distance from too much Internet chat. He gave me his sneering professional look and said, "You look after your egg-laying rabbit, Hajjar."

When Mr. Salman finally visited us, Salsal exploded in anger in front of him, and told him about the rabbit's egg. Mr. Salman ridiculed our story and dismissed our suspicions of Umm Dala. He assured us the woman was honest and had worked with them for years. But Salsal accused him of betrayal and they began to argue, while I sat watching them. From their argument I gathered that in the world of sectarian and political assassinations, people were often betrayed because of greater interests. In many cases the parties in power would hand over hired killers to each other for free, as part of wider deals over political positions or to cover up some large-scale corruption. But Mr. Salman denied all Salsal's accusations. He asked us to calm down, because the assassination of the target would take place in two days. We sat down in the kitchen and Salman explained the plan to us in detail. Then he took two revolvers with silencers out of his bag and said we would be paid right after the operation and that we would then be moved to somewhere else on the edge of the capital.

"A rabbit's egg. Ha, duckling. You're a real joker now," Salman whispered to me before he left.

On the last night I stayed up late with Salsal. I was worried about the rabbit, because it looked like Umm Dala would be on a long holiday. The rabbit would die of hunger and thirst. Salsal was busy with Facebook, as usual. I stayed close to the window, watching the garden. He said he was having a discussion with the Deputy

Minister of Culture on sectarian violence and its roots. I
gathered from Salsal that this minister had been a novelist in Saddam Hussein's time and had written three novels about Sufism. One day he and his wife were at a party
at a wealthy architect's home overlooking the Tigris. His
wife was attractive, stunningly so, and cultured like her
husband. She had a particular interest in old Islamic man-
uscripts. The director of security, a relative of the president, was a guest at the party. After the party was over,
the security chief gave his surveillance section orders to
read our friend's novels. A few days later they threw him
in jail on charges of incitement against the State and the
Party. The director of security bargained with the novelist's wife in exchange for her husband's freedom. When
she rejected his demands, the security chief had one of
his men rape the woman in front of her husband. After
that the woman moved to France and disappeared. They
released the novelist in the mid-nineties and he went off
to look for his wife in France, but he could find no trace of
her. When the dictator's regime fell, he went home and
was appointed Deputy Minister of Culture. The story of
the novelist's life was like the plot of a Bollywood film, but
I was surprised how many details of the man's life Salsal
knew. I felt that he admired the man's personality and
sophistication. I asked him what sect the man was. He
ignored my question. Then I tried to draw him out on the
identity of our target, but Salsal replied that a novice
duckling like me wasn't allowed to know such things. My
only task was to drive the car, and it was Salsal who would
fire the shot, with his silenced revolver.

The next morning we were waiting in front of the

parking garage in the city center. The target was meant to arrive in a red Toyota Crown, and as soon as the car went into the parking garage Salsal would get out of our car, follow him inside on foot, and shoot him. Then we would drive off to our new place on the edge of the capital. That's why I had brought the rabbit along with me and put it in the trunk of the car.

Salsal received a text on his cell phone, and his face turned pale. We shouldn't have had to wait for the target more than ten minutes. I asked him if all was well. He shouted out a curse and slapped his thigh. I was worried. After some hesitation he held out his phone and showed me a picture of a rabbit sitting on an egg. It was a silly Photoshop job. "Do you know who sent the picture?" he asked.

I shook my head.

"The Deputy Minister of Culture," he said.

"What!?!"

"The deputy's the target, Hajjar."

I got out of the car, my blood boiling at Salsal's stupidity and all the craziness of this pathetic operation. More than a quarter of an hour passed, and the target didn't appear. I told Salsal I was pulling out of the operation. He got out of the car too and asked me to be patient and wait a while longer, because both of us were in danger. He got back in the car and tried to contact Salman. I walked to a shop nearby to buy a pack of cigarettes. My heart was pounding like crazy from the anger. As soon as I reached the shop the car blew up behind me and caught fire, burning the rabbit and Salsal to cinders.

An Army Newspaper

TO THE DEAD OF THE IRAN-IRAQ WAR (1980-88)

WE WILL GO TO THE CEMETERY, TO THE MORTUARY, and ask the guardians of the past for permission. We'll take the dead man out to the public garden naked and set him on the platform under the ripe orange sun. We'll try to hold his head in place. An insect, a fly buzzes around him, although flies buzz equally around the living and the dead. We'll implore him to repeat the story to us. There's no need to kick him in the balls for him to tell the story honestly and impartially, because the dead are usually honest, even the bastards among them.

———

Thank you, dear writer, for brushing the fly from my nose and giving me this golden opportunity. I disagree with you only when you try to make the readers frightened of me by describing me as a bastard. Let them judge for themselves, I beg you, and don't you too turn into a rabid dog. Congratulations on being alive! Just don't interfere with the nature of the animal that you are.

Your Honor, ten years ago—that is, before I ended my life—I was working for an army newspaper, supervising the cultural page, which dealt with war stories and poems.

I lived a safe life. I had a young son and a faithful wife who cooked well and had recently agreed to suck my cock every time we had sex. From my work at the newspaper I received many rewards and presents, worth much more than my monthly salary. As the editor will attest, I was the only genius able to enliven the cultural page through my indefatigable imagination in the art of combat. So much so that even the Minister of Culture himself commended me, gave me his special patronage, and promised me in secret that he would get rid of the editor and appoint me in his place. I was not a genius to that extent, nor was I a bastard, as the writer of this story wants to portray me. I was a diligent and ambitious man who dreamt of becoming Minister of Culture and nothing more. To that end I was dedicated in those days to doing my job with honor, as with the sweat of my brow I revised, designed, and perfected my cultural page like a patient baker. No, Your Honor, I was not a censor, as you imagine, because the soldiers who wrote were stricter and more disciplined than any censor I ever met in my life. They would scrutinize every word and examine each letter with a magnifying glass. They were not so stupid as to send in pieces that were plaintive or full of whining and screaming. Some of them wrote because it helped them believe that they would not be killed and that the war was just an upbeat story in a newspaper. Others were seeking some financial or other benefits. There were writers who were forced to write, but all that doesn't interest me now, because at this stage I have no regrets and I am not even afraid. The dead, Your Honor, do not agonize over their crimes and do not long to be happy, as you know. If from time to time we hear the opposite, then those are just trivial religious and poetical exaggerations and ridiculous rumors, which have nothing to do with the real circumstances of the simple dead.

But I do admit that I would often interfere in the structure and composition of the stories and poems, and try as far as possible to add imaginative touches to the written images that would come to us from the front. For God's sake, what's the point, as we are about to embark on war in poetry, of someone saying, "I felt that the artillery bombardment was as hard as rain, but we were not afraid"? I would cross that out and rewrite it: "I felt that the artillery fire was like a carnival of stars, as we staggered like lovers across the soil of the homeland." This is just a small example of my modest interventions.

But the turning point in the story, Your Honor, came when five stories arrived at the newspaper from a soldier who said he had written them in one month. Each story was written in a thick workbook of the colored kind used in schools. On the cover of each workbook the writer had filled in the boxes for name, class, and school, and none of the classes went beyond the elementary level, and each book bore a different name. Each of the stories was about a soldier with the same name as the name written on the cover. The stories were written in a surprisingly elevated literary style. In fact I swear that the world's finest novels, before these stories that I read, were mere drivel, vacuous stories eclipsed by the grandeur of what this soldier had written. The stories did not speak of the war, though the heroes of them were all reluctant soldiers. They were a transparent and cruel exploration of sexual beings from a point of view that was childlike and satanic at the same time. One would read about soldiers in full battle dress, cavorting and laughing with their lovers in gardens and on the banks of rivers; about soldiers who transformed the thighs of prostitutes into marble arches entwined with sad plants the color of milk; soldiers who described the sky in short lascivious sentences as they rested their heads on the breasts of lissome women—magical anthems about bodies that secreted water lilies.

Quickly and with fascination I made inquiries to find out on which front and with which military unit the author of these stories was fighting. I discovered that a few days before the stories were sent, the enemy had made a devastating attack on the army corps with which he was fighting, and the corps had suffered appalling losses in lives and equipment. I had a colleague who worked as an editor on the bravery and medals page in our newspaper, who would shout out whenever he saw me, "You have the brain of a tank, comrade!" I remembered this description of his when I felt the idea flash fully formed in the golden wires of my brain, as I skimmed through these miraculous workbooks. I decided to write the soldier a threatening letter, telling him firmly and frankly that he was liable to interrogation by the Baath party, and perhaps would soon be tried and executed, because his stories were a deliberate and manifest deviation from the party's program in the just war. I relied on the perpetual fear of a soldier, which is widely acknowledged, to persuade him to renounce these stories or apologize to me and beg me bitterly to destroy what he had written, or to forgive him his atrocious act, which he would never repeat. Only then would I know what to do with these sublime stories of humanity. I doubt any great novelist could dream of writing more than five stories displaying such a high level of inventiveness, combining reality and the language of dreams to attain the tenth rank of language, the rank from which fire is created, and from which, in turn, devils are spawned.

Heaven was not far off. It came to my side with lightning speed. One week after my letter to the soldier I received a message from his army corps to say that the soldier had been killed in the latest attack and that no one in his detachment had come out alive. I almost wept for joy at the bounteous gift that destiny had brought as, indescribably elated, I read again the name of the dead soldier.

Your Honor, five months after publishing the first story in my own name (after inventing a distinctive title), I was traveling the countries of the world to present my new story at seminars, where the most famous critics and intellectuals would introduce me. The biggest newspapers and international literary magazines wrote about me. I could not even find enough time to give television and radio interviews. The local critics wrote long studies on how our just war could inspire in man such artistic largesse, such love, such poetry. Many master's and doctoral theses were written in the nation's universities, and in them the researchers endeavored to explore all the insights into poetry and humanity in my story. They wrote about the harmonies between bullets and fate, between the sound of planes and the rocking of a bed, between the kiss and the piece of shrapnel, between the smell of gunpowder and the smell of a woman's vulva, although the story did not make the slightest mention of war, directly or indirectly. When I came home, at a lavish ceremony I was awarded the post of Minister of Culture with no trouble at all. I was in no hurry to publish the four remaining stories, because the first story still had more to yield. I exchanged my wife, my house, my clothes, and my car for new things that I coveted. I can say that I paid homage to the war and raised my hands to heaven in gratitude for the bounty and the priceless gifts. I was confident that the Nobel Prize in Literature would be here on my desk in the ministry after the fifth story. The gates of happiness had opened, as they say.

Then one day three large parcels from the front arrived at my address at the ministry, containing twenty stories sent, it seemed, by the same soldier in the same manner: elementary school books bearing the names of soldiers, containing tales of love and destiny. At first I felt tremendous confusion, which soon turned into icy panic. I quickly picked up the stories and asked the man in charge of the ministry stores to give me the keys to one of the storerooms. I hid them in complete secrecy and made many and intensive contacts to find the soldier. All the messages would come directly to my office in the ministry, and all of them confirmed that the soldier had been killed. They were frightening days. On the following day other parcels arrived, with double the number of stories this time, from the same soldier and in the same manner. Again I carried the stories to the storeroom and put extra padlocks on the door. Cruel months passed, Your Honor, with me torn between hiding the stories, which continued to flood in at an amazing rate, and looking for the

soldier, of whom there was no trace the length and
breadth of the front. In the meantime the second story
had been printed and released. I received phone calls
from the President, the Minister of Defense, and other
state officials, lauding my loyalty and my genius. Invita-
tions from abroad began to flood into the ministry, but
this time I turned them all down on the grounds that the
country was more precious and more important than all
the prizes and conferences in the world, and the country
needed all its righteous citizens in such trying circumstances. In fact I wanted to find a solution to the problem
of the stories, which kept arriving every morning in vast
numbers, like a storm of locusts: today a hundred stories,
tomorrow two hundred, and so on.

Your Honor, I almost lost my "tank brain." At last I
obtained the address of the soldier's house and went to
visit his family to make sure he was dead. His mother told
me she did not believe he was dead. There was only a
small hole in his forehead. It was a sniper's bullet. I took
the address of his grave from his wife and left them some
money. The other storerooms at the ministry were
crammed with workbooks. How would I explain to the
party and the government that I had written all these stories, and why was I writing them in workbooks, and why
the names of the soldiers, seemingly in elementary
school? And why was I storing them this way? There were
dozens of questions, none of which had a logical answer.

I bought some old flour warehouses on the edge of the
city in case more stories poured in. I paid vast amounts to
three workers in the ministry to help dig up the soldier's
grave. There he was with his decayed body and a hole in

his forehead. I shook his body several times to make sure he was dead. I whispered in his ear, then shouted and insulted him. I challenged him, if he could, to open his mouth or move his little finger. But he was dead enough. A worm came out of his neck, chasing another worm, then the two of them disappeared inside again somewhere near his shoulder.

Your Honor, you may not believe this story, but I swear by your omnipotence that within a year the flour warehouses and the ministry storerooms were crammed with the soldier's stories. Of course, I didn't have a chance to read all the stories, but I would take a sample of each batch, and I swear to you that they did not increase only in number, they also became increasingly brilliant and creative. But at the time I trembled and felt that my end would come soon if this flood of stories did not cease. Certainly I left no stone unturned in my inquiries and research. I looked into the addresses from which the parcels were coming. They were being sent in the name of the soldier from various parts of the front, but there was no trace of him. Nevertheless I could not go too far in asking about the parcels, for fear of being exposed.

I went back to the grave and burned the soldier's body. I divorced my second wife and left my job after a psychiatrist helped me by submitting a report saying that my health was deteriorating. I collected all the workbooks from the ministry storerooms and the old flour warehouses and bought some isolated agricultural land, where I built a special incinerator, a large storeroom, a bedroom, and a bathroom, and surrounded it with a high wall. I was sure that the stories would keep pouring in at this new address, but I was prepared for them this time. As I expected, from the morning of the first day at the farm I was working hard day and night, burning the colored workbooks—all the stories, and all the soldier's names—in hopes that the war would end and that this madness of khaki sperm would also stop.

The war did stop, Your Honor, after long and terrifying years, but a new war broke out. The only option left to me was the incinerator fire, as you are the Merciful, the Forgiving.

Your Honor . . .

So now, and before I'm put back in the mortuary, I know you are the Omnipotent, the Wise, the Omniscient, and the Imperious, but did you also once work for an army newspaper? And why do you need an incinerator for your characters?

Crosswords

He wakes up.

It's a mess of a morning.

He hears the words: "For God's sake, I'm going to die of thirst!"

He sits on the edge of the bed. He feels a numbness in his limbs. He pours himself a glass of water. He looks around the ward in a daze. He sees a bird hitting the windowpane. A plump nurse is giving an injection to a man with an arm missing.

"Aha! Cold water! Thank you," says the policeman somewhere deep inside him. . . .

My lifelong friend Marwan used to say, "Across: mankind; down: the sea. The highest mountain peak in the world. A three-letter word. An unfamiliar reality."

They published a picture of him smiling on the cover of the magazine!

It was a picture taken two years ago during the ceremony at which he received the prize for being the best crossword writer. The prize was funded by a billionaire member of Parliament who came back to the country after the change in regime. They say the great passion he acquired for crosswords during his long exile was behind his decision to finance the prize. It was worth fifteen thousand dollars. The prize aroused much envy among certain journalists and writers, who criticized it severely and at length. Marwan won it on merit; I think Marwan could be awarded the title Poet Laureate of Crosswords.

I found some of his old crossword puzzles at the farm once. They contained strange expressions such as "half a moon," "a semi-mythical animal," "a vertical tunnel," "a poisonous grass," and "a half-truth."

In the olden days, when our eyes were like magnifying glasses, the moon was a giant that rose above the rooftops, and we wanted to break it with a stone. In those days Marwan and I were like a single spirit. One autumn evening we lit a fire in a barrel of trash and swore an oath to be forever loyal to each other. We played often, and invented our own secrets, built our own world out of the strangeness of the world around us. We watched the adults' wars on television and saw how the front ate up our elders. Our mothers baked bread in clay ovens and sat down in the sunset hour, afraid and with tears in their eyes. We would steal sweets from shops, climb trees and break our legs and arms. Life and death was a game of running, climbing, and jumping, of watching, of secret dirty words, of sleep and nightmares.

I remember you both well. I felt like a third wheel when we all started high school. I was jealous of you!

Marwan and I would chase the coffins. We would wait for them to reach the turn off the main road. The war was in its fourth year by this point. The coffins were wrapped in the flag and tied firmly to the tops of cars that came from the front. We wanted to be like grown-ups who, when a coffin passed by, would stand and raise their hands solemnly and sadly. We would salute the dead like they did. But when the death car turned a corner, we would race after it down the muddy lanes. The driver would have to slow down so that the coffin didn't fall off. Then the car would choose the door of a sleeping house, and stop in front of it. When the women of the house came out they would scream and throw themselves in the pools of mud and spatter their hair with it. We would hurry to tell our mothers whose house the death car had stopped outside. My mother would always reply, "Go and wash your face," or "Go to Umm Ali next door and ask her if she has a little spice mixture to spare." And in the evening my mother would go and mourn with the local women in the dead man's house, slapping her face and weeping.

Once I was sitting with Marwan waiting for a coffin to arrive. We were eating sunflower seeds. We had waited a long time and were about to give up hope and go back home disappointed. But then the death car loomed on the horizon. We ran after it like happy dogs and were betting on who could beat the car, when it finally stopped in front of Marwan's house. His mother came out screaming hysterically. She ripped her clothes and threw herself in the pool of mud. Bassem, who was standing next to me, stood stock-still and stared in a trance. His big brother noticed him and pulled him into the house. I ran back home, into my mother's arms, crying in torment. "Mummy, my friend Marwan's dad's died," I sobbed. She said, "Wash your face and go to the shop and fetch me half a kilo of onions."

I heard what you wrote yesterday. How the first explosion shredded Marwan's face. The windows shattered and the cupboards fell on top of him. His mouth filled with blood. He spat out teeth and indistinctly heard the screams of his colleague, the editor of the New Woman section. The dust made it impossible to see. She crawled over the rubble screaming, "I'm going to die . . . I'm going to die." Then she fell silent suddenly and forever. Marwan bled a long time and only recovered consciousness in the hospital.

Okay.

Marwan had cute and interesting ideas when we were kids. Once he asked me to help him collect time. We went down toward the valley, stretched out on our stomachs, and proceeded to stare at a weed without moving for more than an hour. We were as silent as stone statues. It was Marwan's belief that if we stared at anything in nature for an hour we would store that hour in our brains. While other people lost time, we would collect it.

It was a double explosion. First they detonated a taxi in front of the magazine's offices. If it hadn't been for the concrete barriers the building would have collapsed. The second vehicle was a watermelon truck, packed with explosives. The first police patrol to arrive after the first explosion brought three policemen. The murderers waited for people to gather and then detonated the second vehicle.

That killed twenty-five people. Two of the policemen were killed on the spot, and their colleague caught fire and began running in every direction. Finally he staggered through the door of the magazine building and collapsed, a lifeless corpse.

In an old text of yours you say:
    A pulp of blood and shit
    a monster
    a defiled planet
    a god-viper
    time spilled in that time.

When we were in high school we used to fuck a prostitute who would give us her customers' shoes. She loved us like a mother. She bought us lots of chocolate and laughed when she slept with us. Marwan used to steal spoons and knives from his house and offer them to her as presents. She was crazy about little knives and addicted to crossword puzzles. We called her "the drunken boat," after the poem by Rimbaud. Before the school year ended, we went on a school trip to explore the mountains. Marwan tried to bring the drunken boat along with us, but the headmaster threatened to expel us from school. On top of a rock shaped like the head of an angry bull, overlooking the valley, we sat down to smoke and read the newspaper. The others went off to explore a cave where prehistoric man had once lived. It was small, like an animal's burrow, and full of spiderwebs, they told us later. I read the paper while Marwan smoked, and then we would switch roles. It was a government newspaper and it was pathetic, from the political news on the front page to the back page devoted to the mysteries of the other world, as if our own world weren't strange and incoherent enough. It was on top of the bull's head that Marwan discovered his vocation. He solved the crossword puzzle in the newspaper in an instant. After that he got a notebook and pen out of his bag and set to work writing his own crossword. He smoked six cigarettes before he finished his first puzzle. It was made up of synonyms from nature. From the rock he stared up at the treetops and said, "Writing crosswords is much easier than solving them."

"Perhaps it's like the real world," I said, blowing smoke and pretending to be a dreamy young man.

"What a philosopher," he said sarcastically. Then he gave an absurd, euphoric yell that filled the valley.

That night he told you that the drunken boat was his relative. Why did he hide this from you for so many years?

We were separated when we went to college. Marwan's family moved to another part of the city. He went to study agriculture, with dreams of ending up with a piece of land where he could plant pomegranate trees. I went to the school of mass communications. We would visit each other constantly, exchange ideas, laugh, and smoke and drink a lot. We would also exchange gossip about the drunken boat. We heard that some pimp had cut off her ear because she stole a ring from a customer who worked in State Security. She got her revenge on him three days later. He was lying asleep on his stomach, so she sank a carving knife deep into his ass. She was given a jail sentence.

Marwan got married in his first year at college. It was passionate love at first sight. The fruit of his love with Salwa was two children, and the fruit came while they were still studying. When they graduated, Salwa stayed at home to look after the children, and Marwan went looking for work. Things weren't easy for someone who had just graduated in agriculture. Meanwhile I started to have articles published on historical esoterica, which I had been writing since I was a student. After I graduated I began work straightaway at a magazine, *Boutique*. We would vent our need to rebel by writing on ideological and social themes. I got in touch with a colleague who was working at the popular magazine *Puzzles* and told him that Marwan was skilled at writing crosswords and astrology columns. Marwan was angry with me for lying about the astrology, but he had no options other than to work at the magazine. He started writing crosswords and even began studying up on astrology.

He sent you a text message that read: Fire Sign—You're compatible with all the signs. Your blood group breathes disappointment and happiness. You stick your tongue in the woman's mouth in order to cool down. The fog that burns on the ceiling is the steam of sweat. You buy pins and colored pictures from the shop. You pin them on your flesh when you receive a guest. The firewood comes to you throughout the night, wrapped in nightmares. When you wake up you have a bath on fire. You eat on fire. You read the newspapers on fire.

You smoke a cigarette on fire. In the coffee cup you come across prophecies of fire. You laugh on fire. You have your lungs checked at the hospital, and they find a spring of errors that looks like a tumor. You dream of the final act: It goes out.

I bought a stuffed scorpion from the toy shop and went to visit Marwan in the hospital. The doctor told me that Marwan's injuries weren't serious. They had extracted some fragments of window glass from his scalp and said he would be fine. Salwa, his wife, was anxious and frightened by Marwan's mental confusion. Like her, I asked the doctor various questions about Marwan's mysterious condition. The doctor asked me, "If you'd gone through a terrorist explosion like that, would you come out laughing and joking?"

"Maybe!" I said, looking at his pointed nose.

He gave me a contemptuous look and took Marwan's wife to one side.

The doctor was wrong; Marwan wasn't suffering just from shock. The burned policeman had got inside him and had taken control of his being. He would say he could hear the policeman's voice in his head, clear and sharp.

Aahh! Perhaps like my voice . . . you frame his sarcastic words and hang them on your living room wall.

War

Peace

God's ass

After coming out of the hospital Marwan kept to himself at home and didn't want to meet any visitors. One day he contacted me and said he wanted to come visit. We bought a bottle of whiskey and went to my apartment. He told me he was reluctant to go to the policeman's house and find out who he was.

He soon got drunk and started shouting and cursing, addressing thin air, saying, "Eat shit," and "Shut up, pimp."

Then he opened his eyes like an owl and threatened to break off our friendship if I didn't believe everything he told me. I took the policeman's address from him and drove him home. Salwa was waiting for us at the window, downcast. Marwan hadn't told her what had happened to him. He was struggling to deal with the disaster himself and was on the verge of madness.

I knocked on the door, and an attractive woman in the spring of her life came out. She was dressed in black, and her eyes were swollen. Standing in the doorway, I saw a little girl playing with a rabbit the same size as she was. I said I was a journalist and I wanted to write an article about the victims of the explosion at *Puzzles* magazine. She said her husband had been killed because of the ignorance that prevailed in this wretched country and she didn't want to speak to anyone. She shut the door. I made discreet inquiries about the young woman's circumstances at a nearby shop. The shopkeeper told me about her husband, the policeman, and how kind he had been and how much he had loved his family. The policeman used to say, "God has blessed me with the three most beautiful women in the world—my mother, my daughter, and my wife. I'm thankful to be alive, however tough it is in this country."

In the three days Marwan spent in the hospital, the policeman told him what had happened: "On the patrol we were telling each other jokes, my colleagues and me. We heard the explosion and headed straight to the *Puzzles* building. My colleagues moved people away from the scene of the incident, and I tried to put out the fire in a car in which a woman and her daughter were burning. Then the second explosion went off.

"My body caught fire. I started to run and scream, then I collapsed in the lobby. I found myself sitting on the ground, a few paces away from my own burning body! I had split in two: one a lifeless corpse, the other shivering from the cold. I ran down the corridors of the magazine building. I saw a woman crawling on her stomach and screaming, but she died before I could do anything. I saw you under the rubble, so I went inside you and I felt warm again. And here I am, smelling what you can smell, tasting what you taste, hearing what you hear, and aware of you as a living being, but I can't see anything. I'm in total darkness. Can you hear me?"

"Yes," Marwan had said.

Okay, this is what you wrote down. . . . Tell me how you reacted to that.

Marwan was angry when I suggested he visit a man of religion. I was bewildered by what he had told me, and it had made me say stupid things. He told me I was crazy and that I was behaving like we were still childhood soul mates. ("It was just a trivial, childish game, you idiot!" he yelled.) Then he started talking to me as calm as a madman: "Do you understand me? Okay, he can share a bed with me, a grave, a window, a seat on the bus, but he's not going to share my body! That's too much; in fact it's complete madness! He grumbles and cries and tells me off as though I'm the thief and it's not him who's stolen my life."

If Marwan went to sleep with only a thin blanket around him, the policeman would wake him up in the middle of the night and say, "I'm cold, Mr. Marwan, please!"

If Marwan drank whiskey, the other guy would complain, "Please, Mr. Marwan, that's wrong. You're burning your soul with that poison! Stop drinking!"

Or, "Why don't you go to the toilet, Mr. Marwan? The gas in your stomach is annoying."

Why couldn't it have been the policeman who incited Marwan to swallow the razor blade?!

Marwan's eyes turned bloodshot from staying up late and drinking too much, and the others got used to his behavior. They treated him as a victim of the explosion. Just another madman. His nerves would flare up for the slightest reason. His colleagues at work didn't abandon him, and he went on devising crosswords, though he stopped writing the horoscopes. He was given a warning when he started writing very difficult crosswords, using words he found in the encyclopedia, or when he wrote, for example, "7 Across: a purple scorpion, 5 Down: a broken womb (six letters, inverted)."

"*This meat tastes salty. What's that horrible smell? Don't you read the Quran? Why don't you pray? The water's hot in the shower.*" *Marwan started to take revenge, taking pleasure in tormenting the policeman. He would eat and drink and do things the policeman didn't like, like drink gallons of whiskey, which the policeman couldn't bear.*

Marwan complained to you about the things that troubled him most. He hadn't gone near his wife's body, except once, three months ago. He had the impression that he was sleeping with her along with another man, and the policeman groaned and wailed like a crazed cat.

The policeman didn't submit to his fate readily. He also knew how much authority he had. Sometimes he would keep jabbering deliriously in Marwan's head until his skull throbbed. The last time Marwan told me about the policeman was while they had a truce.

The policeman wanted Marwan to visit his family. He told him some intimate details of his life so that Marwan would seem like an old friend. Yes, yes, yes. I'm not interested in all those details. When you write, you can choose the limits and call the rest our ignorance.

Marwan sat on the sofa and the policeman's wife brought him some tea, while his mother wiped her tears with the hem of her hijab. Marwan hugged the policeman's little girl as if she were the daughter of a late dear friend.

It was the same scene whenever he visited. He started buying presents for the family on instructions from the

policeman, and Marwan even went to visit the policeman's grave with the family.

The policeman went into a deep silence when he heard
his wife and mother weeping at his grave. He remained
silent for several days. Marwan breathed a sigh of relief
each time, assuming the policeman had disappeared.

*He punched you on the nose when you were driving the car.
I know . . . good . . . details . . . everything in this story is
boring and disgusting.*

Then one day I visited him at his magazine. He was taking swigs from a bottle of arak that he hid in the drawer of
his desk and smoking furiously. I started talking about
our problems working at *Boutique* and the state of the
country, in hopes of calming his nerves. He stopped writing as I spoke.

When I stopped speaking, he stood up and asked if I'd
go with him to visit the drunken boat in prison.

I wasn't even sure she was still alive. I rang the department in charge of women's prisons from his office and
asked after her. They told me she was a patient in the
city's central hospital.

I was extremely uneasy all the way to the hospital.
Marwan smoked a lot and rocked back and forth in his
seat. He began pressing me to take good care of his family,
his voice full of emotion.

I told him, "What are you talking about? Marwan,
what do you mean, 'going to die'? Hey, you're like a cat
with seven good lives left."

He punched me in the nose. Then he lit me a cigarette with his and put it in my mouth. I had an urge to stop the car and give him a thorough beating.

The drunken boat was lying in the intensive care ward. Just a skeleton. She'd been unconscious for a fortnight. We sat close to her on the edge of the bed. Marwan took a small knife shaped like a fish out of his trouser pocket and put it close to her pillow.

He held her hand, and tears flowed down his cheeks.

And after that you came to visit me!

Yes, we bought a range of mezes, two bottles of arak, and twenty cans of beer, and we drove to your farm.

I was so happy to see the two of you! Time had flown, you guys! We had a wild time that night raising a toast to our memories of high school. We put a table out under the lemon tree and cracked open the drinks. Marwan seemed cheerful and relaxed, without any obvious worries. He was laughing and joking, not to mention drinking frantically. Somebody brought up that boy at school called "the genius." He was an eccentric student who had memorized all the textbooks within months. The teachers were convinced he was a genius, and they were shocked when he got poor grades on the final exams, barely enough to qualify to study at the oil institute. In his first year of college, he sneaked in at night and set fire to the lecture hall, then shot himself with a revolver. It was all a bit of a tragedy!

You told us at length about your days of isolation on your farm, where you wanted to be free to write a book on the history of decapitation in Mesopotamia.

The conversation eventually flagged, and we started to slur our words. We were drunk, and Marwan fell back into a deep silence. We got up to go into the house. Marwan asked me to recite whatever I could remember by Pessoa, his favorite writer.

I'm not me, I don't know anything,
I don't own anything, I'm not going anywhere,
I put my life to sleep
In the heart of what I don't know.

It was a wonderful summer night. Three best friends from school reunited. I lay on the grass, looked up at the clear sky, and began to imagine God as a mass of shadows. We heard Marwan's screams coming from the bathroom. We couldn't save him. He died in the pool of blood he had vomited.

You phoned me a week later, and we went to an art exhibition in my car. We were going along the highway when, by mistake, I overtook a truck loaded with rocks.

Enough, God keep you.

What, you're tired!

I want to sleep awhile.

Okay, let's sleep.

I hope that when I wake up I can't hear you anymore and you're completely out of my life.

Me too, you fuck.

The Hole

1

I was stuffing the last pieces of chocolate into the bag. I had already filled my pockets with them. I took some bottles of water from the storeroom. I had enough canned salmon, so I hid the remaining cans under the pile of toilet paper. Then, just as I was heading for the door, three masked gunmen broke in. I opened fire and one of them fell to the ground. I ran out the back door into the street, but the other two started to chase me. I jumped over the fence of the local soccer field and ran toward the park. When I reached the far end of the park, down by the side of the Natural History Museum, I fell into a hole.

———

"Listen, don't be frightened."

His hoarse voice scared me.

"Who are you?" I asked him, paralyzed by fear.

"Are you in pain?"

"No."

"That's normal. It's part of the chain."

The darkness receded when he lit a candle.

"Take a deep breath! Don't worry!"

He gave an unpleasant laugh, full of arrogance and disdain.

His face was dark and rough, like a loaf of barley bread. A decrepit old man. His torso was naked. He was sitting on a small bench, with a dirty sheet on his thighs. Next to him there were some sacks and some old junk. If he hadn't moved his head like a cartoon character, he would have looked like an ordinary beggar. He was tilting his head left and right like a tortoise in some legend.

"Who are you? Did I fall down a hole?"

"Yes, of course you fell. I live here."

"Do you have any water?"

"The water's cut off. It'll come back soon. I have some marijuana."

"Marijuana? Are you with the government or the opposition?"

"I'm with your mother's cunt."

"Please! Is the place safe?"

He lit a joint and offered it to me. I took a drag and examined him. He looked suspicious. He smoked the rest of the joint and tuned a radio beside him to a station that was playing a song in a strange language. It sounded like some African religious beat.

"Are you foreign?"

"Can't you tell by my accent? I'm speaking your language, man! But you can't speak my language, because I was in the hole before you. But you'll speak the language of the next person who falls in."

"Ah, man. I hate the way you talk."

He looked away, leaned his tortoise-like neck forward,

and lit another candle. I could see the place more clearly now. There was a dead body. I examined it in the candle-light, a bitter taste in my mouth. It was the body of a sol-dier, and there was an old rifle nearby. His legs were lacerated, possibly by some sharp piece of shrapnel. He looked like a soldier from ancient times.

"It's true, it's a Russian soldier."

He'd read my thoughts, and on his face there was an artificial smile.

"And what was he doing in our country? Was he work-ing at the embassy?"

"He fell in the forest during the winter war between Russia and Finland."

"You really are mad."

"Listen, I don't have time for the likes of you. I wanted to be polite with you, but now you're starting to get on my nerves. I'm in a shitty mood today."

I began to examine the hole. It was like a well. Its walls were of damp mud, but the pores in the mud gave off a sharp, acrid smell. Maybe the smell of flowers! I lifted up the candle to try to see how deep the hole was. At the mouth, the lights in the park were visible.

"Do you believe in God?" he asked me in his disgust-ing voice.

"We're always in his care. Pray to him, man, to spare us the disasters of life."

He rounded his hands into the shape of a megaphone and started to shout hysterically, "O Lord of Miracles, Almighty One, Omniscient One, God, Great One, send down a giraffe or a monkey as long as it's a hundred eighty cen-timeters tall! Make something other than a human fall in the hole! Make a dry tree fall in the hole! Throw us four snakes so we can make a rope out of them!"

As if the craziness of this tortoise-like old man was what I needed! I humored him with his sarcastic prayer and said that if another man fell down the hole it would be easy to get out of it, because it wasn't deep.

"You're right, and here's a third man!" he said, pointing at the Russian soldier.

"But he's dead."

"Dead here, but not in another hole."

The old man suddenly pulled out a knife. I watched him warily, in case he attacked me. He crawled on his knees toward the body of the soldier and started cutting out chunks of flesh and eating them. He paid no attention to me, as if I didn't exist.

2

That night I had picked up my revolver before heading out to the shop. I'd closed the place down months before, when the killing and looting started to spread across the capital. I would drop by the shop now and then when it was hard to get food or water from any of the shops near our house. The economy had quickly collapsed, and things had grown even worse due to the strikes. There were signs of an uprising, and chaos spread in the wake of the government's resignation. The first protests began in the capital, and within a few days panic and violence swept the country. Bands of people occupied all the government buildings. They formed interim committees and attempted to govern. However, things suddenly turned sour again. People said that it was businessmen who backed the organized gangs that managed to take control of the northern part of the country. The rich and the supporters of the fugitive government were convinced that the new faith-based groups would come to power and impose their obscurantist ideology. That's what the spokesman for the northern region said, and he also threatened that the region would secede. The extremists in the faith-based groups took no interest in speeches by politicians or revolutionaries. They were working silently behind the scenes, and in one shock assault they seized control of the country's nuclear missile base. "Mankind has led us into ruination, so let's go back to the wisdom of the Creator." That was their motto.

As for the army, it fought on several fronts. In the country's main port, soldiers with machine guns killed more than fifty people who were trying to rob the main bank. People started to confront the army, which they began to see as the enemy of change. There was plenty of weaponry. Our southern neighbors were said to have given weapons to civilians. In the capital some sensible people called for calm and for a way out of the storm that was sweeping the country. The army surrounded the missile base and began negotiating with the extremist leader, who was living among armed tribes in another country. He was a colonel who had been expelled from the army because of his extremist ideas. It was also said that he had a slogan tattooed on his forehead: PURGE THE EARTH OF DEVILS.

The old man chewed the meat and went back to his place as if he'd just finished eating a sandwich. He wiped his mouth with a dirty towel, pulled out a book, and began to read. I took out a bar of chocolate and devoured it nervously. The old man was quite loathsome and disgusting.

He looked up from his book and said, "Listen, I'll get straight to the point. I'm a jinni." He put out his hand for me to shake.

I looked at him inquisitively.

What was it my grandfather had said in his last few weeks? He kept raving in front of the pomegranate tree (all he could do in this world was suck pomegranates and stare at the tree).

How I wanted to get up and kick the old man. I noticed he was looking at me spitefully and smiling in a way that suggested contempt. Then he said, "You seem to be braver and less disgusting than this Russian. Listen, I'm not interested in you and the people who visit the hole. All I'm looking for in your stories is amusement. When you spend your life in this endless chain, the pleasure of playing is the only thing that keeps you going. Wretches like this Russian remind me of the absurdity of the game. The romance of fear transforms the chain into a gallows. As soon as our friend the Russian fell in the hole, it terrified him that I was in it. He aimed his rifle at my head. And when I told him I was a jinni, he almost went crazy. He had one bullet. If it didn't kill me, he would die of fright, and if he didn't fire it he would remain hostage to his own paranoia."

"Very well, and what happened?"

"Ha! I told him I knew all the secrets of his life, and to make him more frightened I said I knew Nikolai, his aunt's youngest son. The soldier was disturbed when he heard the name. I talked about how he and Nikolai raped a girl in his village. He broke down and fired a bullet at my head. It's a silly chain, full of your human stories. Would you believe sayings such as this?" He read from his book: "'We are merely exotic shadows in this world.' Trite talk, isn't it? Life is beautiful, my friend. Enjoy it and don't worry. I used to teach poetry in Baghdad. I think it's going to rain. One day we might know one of the secrets or how to get out. There's no difference here. What matters is the music of the chain."

I shouted, "You're eating a corpse, you disgusting old man!"

"Ha! You'll eat me too, and they'll eat you or use you as material for their batteries or for drinking."

I punched him in the face and shouted again: "If you weren't an old man, I'd smash your skull in, you bastard!"

He paid no attention to what I said. All he said was that there was no need for me to be upset, because he would leave the hole soon and I would fall into another hole from another time. He said his book would stay with me. It's a book full of hallucinations. It has detailed explanations of the secret energy extracted from insects to create additional organs to reinforce the liver, the pancreas, the heart, and all the body's other organs.

3

Before leaving the hole, the old man told me he was from Baghdad and had lived in the time of the Abbasid caliphate. He had been a teacher, a writer, and an inventor. He suggested to the caliph that they light the city streets with lanterns. He had already supervised the lighting of the mosques and was now busy on his plan to expand the house lighting system by more contemporary methods. The Baghdad thieves were upset by his lanterns, and one day they chased after him after dawn prayers. Close to his home the lantern man tripped on his cloak and fell down the hole.

One of the things this Baghdadi told me was that everyone who visits the hole soon learns how to find out about events of the past, the present, and the future, and that the inventors of the game had based it on a series of experiments they had conducted to understand coincidence. There were rumors that they couldn't control the game, which rolls ceaselessly on and on through the curves of time. He also said, "Anyone who's looking for a way out of here also has to develop the art of playing; otherwise they'll remain a ghost like me, happy with the game. . . . Ha, ha, ha. I'm fed up with trying to decipher symbols. There are two opponents in every game. Each one has his own private code. It's a bloody fight, repetitive and disgusting. The rest is memory, which they can't erase easily. In your day, experiments with memory were in their infancy. The scientists went on working for more than a century and a half after those first attempts, the purpose of which was to discover the memory centers in rats' brains. It turned out that the rats remembered what they learned even if their brains had been completely destroyed in the laboratory. Those would be amazing experiments if they were applied to humans. Is memory a winning card in this game that we play so seriously till it's all over, or should we merely have fun? Everyone that falls down here becomes a meal or a source to satisfy the instincts, or energy for other systems. We who . . . damn, who are we? No one knows!"

The old man died and left me really helpless. Day had broken and snowflakes fell from the mouth of the hole. The Russian's body looked ghostly. I wanted to reach back to other times I might have lived in, the traces of which are scattered to places I previously thought imaginary. My consciousness was moving like a roller coaster at an amusement park. I watched the snowflakes swirling. The vision of the soldier had disappeared. My eyes were open and my mind was asleep. I may have been sleeping for hundreds of years. I imagined a dead cell. Am I really just in my mind or in every cell in my body? A strong smell of flowers filled the hole. I closed my eyes, but then a young girl fell into the hole. She was carrying on her back an electronic bag tied around her chest with many straps, and to her thighs were tied metallic phosphorous clusters. In her hand she was holding something that looked like an electronic gauge.

"Who are you?" she asked me, panting. There were wounds disfiguring her pretty face.

"I'm a jinni. What happened to you?"

I felt as if my voice went back to ancient times.

"A blood analysis robot was chasing me," she said.

She was sucking her finger, which was swollen like a mushroom.

"That's normal," I said apathetically, then crawled toward the corpse of the old man.

The Madman of Freedom Square

IN THOSE UNFORGETTABLE DAYS BEFORE THE MIRACLE happened and I discovered the truth that everyone now denies or ignores, we used to guard the platform where the two statues stood. We had light arms, three mortars, and seven RPG launchers. The prominent people and opinion-makers in the neighborhood had rejected an order from the new government to remove the statues, and we had information that the army would storm the neighborhood by night. While deep down I didn't consider this to be my battle, it was much easier to deceive myself than to bear the shame of running away. The battle might break out at any moment and I might lose my life for the sake of these two young men cut from stone who stood upright on the dais as though they were about to fall flat on their faces. It's clear that the sculptor was just a building worker who knew nothing of the art of sculpture. The fanatical Islamists had a fatwa that all the statues in the country should be removed because they were idols and incompatible with Islamic law. As for the government, it had decided to remove everything that symbolized the period of the former dictatorial regime.

The notables and other people of the neighborhood held the view that the statues had nothing to do with the former regime nor with repressive fatwas. I didn't believe in that kind of nonsense. My father said it was a symbolic battle of destiny for the sake of the neighborhood's future. I don't know how my father, as a science teacher at the high school, could believe such superstitions. Of course, there are dozens of versions of the statues story, but perhaps the version that my grandfather told was the one closest to the truth. The touch of realism in my grandfather's story made the people of the neighborhood seem even more naive, whereas his intention was to portray them as friendly, intelligent, and generous. This is what I was thinking at the time, before my life changed forever.

Perhaps it would be best if I first repeated to you in brief my grandfather's version of the story, before I tell you what happened to me on the night of the battle. With great sadness he would say, "No one knows when exactly the two young men appeared. They were the same age, the same height, and as alike as twins. People in the neighborhood thought they were from those rich districts far away, but they could not guess where they were going. Each of them carried a backpack, and they wore smart clothes suggesting they were wealthy and well bred. What struck the people of the neighborhood most was their blond hair and their white complexions. The Darkness district was one of the most wretched in the city, and the inhabitants were skinny with swarthy complexions they had inherited from their peasant ancestors. It was the people in nearby parts of the city who gave the name Darkness to the neighborhood, the only one that did not have electricity. I imagine it was the first time the people of the neighborhood had seen visitors of this species of humanity.

"Every morning the two young men would walk through the village toward the river in the distance, coming from the direction of the wasteland that separates the Darkness district from the Arbanjiya district. They would smile tenderly and with affection at the half-naked children of the neighborhood, and greet the elders with a slight nod that suggested respect. They would avoid the muddy patches in the lanes simply and unassumingly, without showing signs of disgust or haughtiness. The people of the neighborhood saw them as angels from heaven. Nobody spoke to them or asked them any intrusive questions, or stood in their way for any reason whatsoever. The neighborhood was dazzled by the aura of light that radiated from the young men. They would walk with confident, measured steps, as though they had learned to walk in a private school. Their silence added to the mystery of them. They were well mannered and dignified, but with a light touch of good humor. The people of the neighborhood fell in love with the two young men and grew accustomed to their radiant appearance every morning. Day by day people became more and more attached to the two handsome youths, and their coming and going became like the rising and the setting of the sun. The children were the first to grow attached to them: They would gather early in the morning on the edge of the quarter to wait for the young men to appear from across the wasteland. They would bet Sinbad cards on which lane the men would come down today. When "the blonds" arrived the children would be thrilled. The children would tag along with them until they reached the other side of the neighborhood, jumping up around them, laughing, and touching the young men's clothes with their fingertips, in a mixture of fear and exhilaration. The children would be even happier when the men would graciously bend down, without stopping walking, to let the children touch their blond hair. The girls of the neighborhood fell for the blonds, and before long it was as though a sacred and secret covenant had been concluded between them and the local people.

"The days passed without either side daring to break the barrier of silence or ambiguity. Before the blonds appeared it would have been suicide for a stranger to enter the neighborhood. But now the girls would stick their heads out from the balconies and windows to feast their eyes on the beauty of the two young men and sigh with the ardent passion of youth. As soon as the men were gone they would drift off in daydreams as they listened to love songs on the radio. When the blonds were coming, the girls would take their radios out on the balcony in hopes that the radio station would play a love song at just that moment, and if a love song was on they would turn the volume right up as though the song were a personal message of love from the girl with the radio. The two young men would react to all this respectfully, modestly, and amiably.

"The days passed." My grandfather gave a deep sigh and prolonged the *a* of "passed."

"An old woman died," my grandfather said. "And fifty children were born in the neighborhood, of skinny mothers and unemployed fathers. The summer passed and the men who sell vegetables made more money. The local women attributed to the baraka or spiritual power of the blonds the fact that their husbands, who worked sweeping the streets or as school janitors in the city center, had all received pay raises. The husbands, who had been skeptical about the baraka of the two men, soon stopped scoffing, when the government decided to install electricity at the beginning of winter. After all these signs of baraka, the women began a campaign to plant flowers outside their front doors so that the blonds could smell the fragrance as they made their angelic passage through the Darkness district. As for the men, they filled in the puddles so the blonds would not have to walk around them.

"There was a spark of hope in the faces of the people, and this brought out their natural color, which in the past had been coated with the grime of sadness and misery. Everyone started to make sure the children were clean, sewed new clothes for them, and told them to be more polite when they met the blonds. They taught them a lovely song about birds and spring to sing when they were with the blonds.

"To reinforce all this veneration and faith, a man in the neighborhood was suddenly appointed to an important position in the government, and he promised to pave the streets and extend the pipes to bring in drinking water. The young people told the man to ask the government to bring telephone lines to the Darkness district, and I also remember what the people did when they found out that a group of evildoers were planning to attack the blonds close to the river. They had a discussion in the mayor's house and then warned the evildoers that they and their families would be thrown out of the neighborhood if they went ahead with their plans, and the bad guys backed down.

"No more than two years after the blonds first appeared, every wish had come true, just as miracles happen in myths and legends. The old maids got married, the muddy lanes were paved, everyone with a chronic disease was cured, most of the children passed their exams, whereas previously their results had been embarrassing. The biggest miracle of all was the overthrow of the monarchy through a coup by heroic officers who enjoyed the support of the people. It's clear that all this good fortune and felicity had come to the people by virtue of the blonds. From then on harmony and love reigned among the people of the neighborhood, and enmity and violence almost disappeared. Another new thing was that the schools became mixed, with boys and girls together, and the government built a clinic close to the neighborhood, and I used to sell chickpeas in front of it. The government did something very logical when it changed the name from the Darkness district to the Flower district. It chose the new name after a government official visited the neighborhood and submitted a report in which he mentioned how many flowers there were and also how clean the neighborhood was. Almost every house had a telephone line, and it was noticeable that more than a few of the inhabitants had come to have cars. The other new thing in the neighborhood was that the old people now took part in the adult literacy program and were enthusiastic

about discovering the mysteries of the alphabet and of
language in general. In short the neighborhood acquired
a new vitality and prosperity after the medicine began to
take effect. But the happiness evaporated on that ill-fated
morning, the day after the military coup, when the children went out to the edge of the neighborhood to wait for
the blonds to come. They waited long and the blonds did
not come. Their mothers joined them and sat with them
on the wasteland. The government had built a wide road
across the middle of the wasteland and now tanks and
armored personnel carriers were driving along it. Then
the rest of the local people came along to join them, and
everyone was looking at the tanks on the main road,
belching out black smoke. They had a sense of bitterness
inside them, lumps in their throats and tears in their eyes.

"The sun had set and darkness had descended again."

My grandfather blew out the lantern flame and gave a
long sigh.

———

It was after midnight, and the new government's tanks
were invading the neighborhood to remove the statues of
the blonds. The men of the neighborhood had taken up
battle positions on the roofs of the houses and in the alley-
ways. A fierce battle broke out, and even the women took
part. I had slipped through, along with three friends carrying grenade launchers to destroy a tank that was moving down the middle of the main road, but the helicopters
firing from above restricted our movements. We hid
behind a taxi parked on the pavement. Then some of the
shops and other buildings caught fire. It looked like we
were doomed to lose the battle because of the constant

bombardment from the helicopters. We broke one of the windows of the taxi and hid inside, with plans to drive it off and escape. Suddenly one of the helicopters in the sky burst into flames and crashed onto the roofs of the houses. Then our fighters hit a tank with their missiles, and we saw the government troops withdrawing in panic. A while later we saw a group of young men from the neighborhood rushing forward like madmen, shouting "Allahu akbar" and spraying bullets around at random, jubilant and heedless of the battle. We got out of the taxi when the young men went by, and we heard from them that God had brought about a miracle. They told us the blonds had come back to the neighborhood and were now fighting ferociously against the government forces. They said it was the blonds alone who had set fire to the tank and brought down the helicopter. My friends cheered and shouted "Allahu akbar" with the group as they ran toward the government troops, firing bullets in every direction. This neighborhood was surely just a vast mental hospital. I felt anger and hatred as I stood by the taxi, transfixed, watching the throngs celebrating the miraculous victory. I lit a cigarette and thought that the best way to end my torment would be to abandon this cave they call the Darkness district. Just as I turned to walk home, a torrent of missiles suddenly rained down right across the neighborhood. One of these missiles threw me and the wreckage of the taxi against a nearby wall. I saw flames around me on all sides. I did not feel any pain, but the sudden silence around me gave me a strange feeling of peace. When the blonds pulled me from under the wreckage of the car I saw that one of them was wearing a shirt stained with my blood. My father says I was unconscious when they found me in front of the door to our house, but I'm sure the blonds carried me on a white stretcher, and all along the way they smiled at me, and I reached out my hand to touch their beautiful blond hair.

Some of the young men from the new generation in the neighborhood now call me the madman of Freedom Square. The government planted some trees and put some benches where the statues of the blonds had stood. They put up a large plaque with the new name of the neighborhood: Freedom district. I know what these idiots say. They claim that the piece of shrapnel that went into my head damaged my brain. But they are just villagers still living in the Dark Age. I have repeatedly asked the notables and others to contribute money to rebuild the statues of the blonds and protect the history of the neighborhood. This is the least I could do to repay them the favor of saving my life. What makes me angry is that even my father no longer believes in the story of the blonds, after the soldiers demolished the statues and killed many young men that night. Some people now claim that the story of how the blonds miraculously appeared that night and fought on our side is just cheap propaganda, spread by certain youngsters to raise the morale of our fighters, and that the government army wiped out the resistance before morning broke. But I am quite sure it was the blonds who carried me on the white stretcher, and with these very fingers of mine I touched their angelic hair.

A few days ago I met a stranger whom I believe to be honest, not a fake like most of the people in the neighborhood, and he told me he believed my story of how the

blonds appeared that night. He spoke to me at length
about how we have lost our history and heritage because
of the agents of the West and because we have neglected
our religion, and how freedom means not becoming stooges
in the hands of the infidels, but what I don't fully understand is the wide belt the man wrapped around my waist
in his house this morning. I feel very hot because the belt
is so heavy. I'll sit down in the shade of the tree. . . . Damn,
the women and children have taken all the benches.

The Iraqi Christ

WE WERE MEANT TO CAMP IN AN OLD GIRLS' SCHOOL, AND some of the soldiers decided the best place to spend the night was the school's air-raid shelter. Daniel the Christian picked up his blanket and other bedding and headed out into the open courtyard.

"Of course, Chewgum Christ is crazy," remarked one of the soldiers, a man as tall as a palm tree, his mouth stuffed with dry bread.

"Perhaps he doesn't want to sleep with us Muslims," suggested another soldier.

The young men were monkeys. They didn't know the truth about Daniel. They were too busy masturbating on the benches in the classrooms where the girls used to sit. Just one missile and they would shortly be charred pricks. In absurd wars such as this one, Daniel's gift was a lifesaver. We had been together in the Kuwait war, and if it hadn't been for his amazing powers we wouldn't have survived. Aside from his gloomy nature, Daniel could hardly be considered ordinary flesh and blood. He was a force of nature.

I spread out my blanket close to him and lay on my back, like him, staring into space.

"Go to sleep, Ali, my friend. Go to sleep. There's no sign tonight. Go to sleep," he said to me, and started snoring straightaway.

Daniel was always chewing gum. The soldiers had baptized him Chewgum Christ. I often imagined that Daniel's chewing was like an energy source, recharging the battery that powered the screen in his brain. His life's dream was to work in the radar unit. He had completed high school and volunteered to join the air force, but his application was rejected, maybe because his father had been a prominent communist in the seventies. He loved radar the way other men love women or soccer. He collected pictures of radar systems and talked about signals and frequencies as though he was talking about a romp in the hay with some girlfriend. During the last war, I remember him saying, "Ali, humans are the best radar receivers, compared with other animals. You just need to practice making your spirit leave your body and then bring it back, like exhaling and inhaling." He had tattooed on his right arm the radar equation:

$$P_r = \frac{P_t G_t A_r \sigma F^4}{(4\pi)^2 R_t^2 R_r^2}$$

After Daniel's hopes of joining the air force were dashed, he volunteered for the medical corps. But he did not give up his passion for radar, and anyone who knew him would not have been surprised by this obsession, because Chewgum Christ was himself the strangest radar in the world. I remember those terrifying nights during the war over Kuwait. The soldiers, as frightened as ducklings, would follow him wherever he went. The coalition planes would be bombing our trenches, and we wouldn't be able to fire a single shot back. We felt like we were fighting some ultimate, almighty force. All we could do was dig more trenches and scamper from place to place like rats. In the end we camped near the desert. All we had left was our faith in God and the powers of Daniel the Christian. One night we were eating in the trench with the other soldiers when Daniel started complaining of a stomachache. The soldiers stopped eating, picked up their weapons, and prepared to stand, all of them looking at Daniel's mouth.

"I want to lie down in the shade of the large water tank," Christ said finally.

The soldiers joined him as he left the trench, jostling to keep close to him as if he were a shield against missiles. They sat around him in the shade. Just thirty-five minutes later three bombs fell on the trench. It wasn't the only time. Christ's premonitions saved many soldiers. In Daniel's company the war played out like the plot of a cartoon. In the blink of an eye, reality lost cohesion. It fell apart and you started to hallucinate. What could one make, for example, of the way a constant itching in Daniel's crotch foretold that an American helicopter would crash on the headquarters building? Is it credible that three successive sneezes from Daniel could foretell a devastating rocket attack? They fired them at us from the sea. We soldiers were like sheep, fighting comic book wars.

I heard many rumors that reports on Christ had been submitted to the Supreme Command. But the chaos of those days and the defeat of our army, which was crushed like flies, prevented the authorities from paying any attention. There were many stories about the President's interest in magicians, the occult, and people with prodigious powers. They claim it was at his suggestion that so many books on parapsychology were unexpectedly translated in Iraq in the eighties, because he had heard that the advanced countries were developing telepathic techniques and using them for espionage. The President thought that science and the occult were one and the same; they just used different methods to reveal the same secrets.

Christ was not boastful about his premonitory powers and did not consider them unusual. He used to tell stories from history about mankind's ability to foretell the future. I came to the conclusion that Daniel's melancholia made it impossible for him to take pleasure in the talent he possessed. Even his interest in radar did not bring him pleasure. His ideas about happiness were mysterious. I understood from him that he was frightened by some inner gloom. He thought his talent was just another sign of how impotent and insignificant we are in this mysterious world. He told me that at an early age he read a story by an Iraqi writer whose personality was simultaneously sarcastic and fearful. The hero in the story was swallowed by a shark after a fierce battle in the imaginary river of time. The hero sits trapped in the darkness there and thinks alone, "How can I reconcile my private life with my awareness that a world is collapsing in front of my eyes?"* "That's a question that has weighed on my life. It has kept me awake like an open wound," said Christ.

When we woke up the next day the American forces

* As Ingmar Bergman once asked in an interview.

had reached the outskirts of Baghdad. A few hours later they brought down the statue of the dictator. It was a surreal shock. We put on civilian clothes and went back to our families. It was just another war of the blind in which no one in our squadron fired a single shot.

After it was all over, I met Daniel several times. He had gone back to live with his elderly mother. When chaos broke out in the country, I visited him in their house in Baghdad. I wanted to speak to him about going back to the army. He said he had hated the dictator, but he would not contribute to an army under the auspices of the occupier. After that I didn't meet him again. I myself returned to the army, and Daniel went back to looking after his mother. He had two sisters who had migrated to Canada years before, and his other relatives had left the country one by one, driven away by wars and the madness of sectarian fanaticism. Of his large family, only his mother remained. I found out that Daniel spent most of his time at home reading novels and encyclopedias, following the news and caring for his mother, who had lost her hearing, her sight, and her memory. Old age isolated her from the world. The old woman was incontinent. Christ would change her diapers every few hours. His mother's death would sever the thread that tied him to the place. He didn't plan to emigrate. In a long letter, his older sister implored him to leave the country, but Christ was as stubborn as his mother. Both of them rejected the devil's temptation—to abandon their lost paradise.

After mass one Sunday, Christ took his mother to a local restaurant famous for its kebabs. He liked the cleanliness of the place and the way it set aside seats for children. The restaurant had changed greatly. He couldn't remember the last time he had been there. Christ chose an empty table in the corner and helped his mother to sit down. The waiter's good humor cheered him up. The man would mix up the names of the dishes with the names of daily instruments of slaughter. The customers laughed and loved him. He would call out orders such as "One explosive, mind-blowing, gut-wrenching kebab. One fragmentation stew. Two ballistic rice and beans."

Christ asked for one and a half orders of kebab with hot peppers, a glass of ayran,* and a cold juice. The waiter came back with the order and made a joke about inquisitive people. Christ smiled politely. He picked up his mother's fingers gently and placed them down to feel the hot kebabs and the grilled tomatoes. Then he put them back in place on the edge of the table. He picked up a tasty morsel and pressed it into her mouth, smiling at her with extraordinary, selfless love.

A young man asked if he could sit down at Christ's table. Stocky in build and with a hard expression on his face, he was probably about twenty. He ordered a kebab with extra onions. He was actually quite handsome but was scratching his neck incessantly, like someone with scabies. His eyes shifted from table to table. Daniel moved the plate of salad closer to his mother's fingers and left her to feel out the vegetables on the plate. He prepared another mouthful for her. The young man watched them stealthily. He seemed eccentric. He kept chewing his

---

* Ayran: a cold beverage of yogurt mixed with ice water and sometimes salt.

piece of meat and trying to swallow it, as tears streamed from his beautiful eyes. Daniel was wary of him. He leaned forward and asked if he could help. He repeated the question, but the young man kept his eyes on his plate and did not seem to have heard Daniel. He kept chewing, and his tears flowed. He took out a handkerchief, wiped away his tears, and cleaned his nose. He looked around the restaurant, then stared into Christ's eyes. His features changed to reveal another face, as though he had taken off a mask. He grasped the flap of his jacket and pulled it aside like someone baring his chest.

"It's an explosive belt. One word from you and I'll blow myself up," the young man said, with a threatening glance toward the old woman.

———

I was killed by friendly fire, myself. We were on a joint patrol with the American forces after the invasion. Someone opened fire on us from a house in the village. The Americans responded hysterically, thinking we had opened fire on them. I was shot three times in the head. I met Christ in our next world, and we were overjoyed. He told me how he was inexplicably drawn to that young man in the kebab restaurant. It wasn't just terror that had paralyzed him, but also some mysterious desire for salvation. For some moments he stared into the young man's face. The man leaned toward him and asked him to stand up and go to the bathroom with him. At first he didn't budge from his place, as if turned to stone. Then he kissed his mother's head and stood up.

The young man led the way to the toilets. He closed the door and kept the tip of his finger on the button on the explosive belt. With his other hand he pulled a pistol out of his belt and pointed it at Daniel's head. The young man was practically hugging Christ by this point, wrapping his arms around him because the space was so tight. He summed up what he wanted: Daniel should wear the explosive belt in his place, in exchange for him saving the old woman's life.

The young man was in a hysterical state and could hardly control himself. He said there would be someone filming the explosion from outside the restaurant and that if he didn't blow himself up they would kill him. Daniel said nothing in response. They started to sweat. One of the customers tried to push open the restroom door. The young man cleared his throat. Then he again promised Christ he would take the old woman safely out of the restaurant, but if Daniel didn't blow himself up he would kill her. Half a minute of silence passed, then he agreed with a nod of his head and stared blankly into the young man's eyes. The young man asked him to undo the belt and wrap it around his own waist. It was a difficult process because the room was so narrow. The young man withdrew cautiously, leaving Christ in the bathroom with the explosive belt on. Then he rushed toward the old woman in the corner of the restaurant. He tapped her gently on the shoulder and took hold of her hand. She stood up and followed him like a child. The restaurant had started to fill up, and the noise level was rising, as people laughed and the cutlery clattered like a sword fight.

Christ fell to his knees. He could hardly breathe, and he pissed in his trousers. He opened the bathroom door and crawled into the restaurant. Someone met him at the door and ran back shouting, "A suicide bomber, a suicide bomber!"

Amid the panic, as men, women, and children trampled on each other to escape, Christ saw that his mother's chair was empty, and he pressed the button.

A Thousand and One Knives

1

At noon Jaafar the referee was waiting at the end of the lane, his army binoculars around his neck and a soccer ball in his lap. The boys arrived one after another and surrounded him, joking with him and talking excitedly about the striker on the Sector 32 team. Jaafar reassured them. "We have Allawi al-Saba. He's the Messi of Sector Twenty-nine," he said.

The boys took turns pushing Jaafar's wheelchair. One of them said, "The Sector Thirty-two team might bring a referee of their own."

Jaafar wasn't bothered. He told them he knew how to handle that. They reached the field, Jaafar threw the ball, and the boys ran after it.

Jaafar was forty-five years old, but he was still young at heart. With his passion for sports, his dynamism, and his determination, he amazed his friends and his few enemies. He had been the most famous pool player in Sector 29, and when he was an army deserter the military police couldn't catch him. He was like a fox, but his addiction to

pool halls was his downfall. One evening the military
police surrounded him at the Khorasan pool hall in
Karada, where he used to take on the most famous players
in the area. They sent him off to the Kuwait war, and when
he came back both his legs had been amputated. Jaafar
was a good lad, one of the boys—that's how the people of
the sector saw him. But some of them found fault with his
passion for soccer and the way he hung out with the local
youth at his age. Jaafar didn't take much notice of such
talk, because the young had to learn the basics of the game.
He would organize matches for them and act as referee.
He would remind his critics of the famous national squad
player who came from Sector 29 and whom he claimed to
have trained, adding each time, "A miracle that will save
the whole country will be my doing too!"

On the edge of the soccer field there was a large Dump-
ster that gave off white smoke with a putrid stench that
drifted over the playing area. Women, some in abayas and
some without, came out of the houses around the field
with bags of trash. Jaafar watched them through his binoculars while the boys ran after the ball, shouting. With
his binoculars Jaafar also watched the boys playing.

The Sector 32 team arrived, accompanied by a young
man with a beard, and he and Jaafar agreed that Jaafar
would referee the first half and the other man the second
half. The match began. Jaafar pushed his wheelchair up
and down the field at high speed in a frenzied passion. He
shouted at the boys, either to encourage them or to repri-
mand them, and when they were too far off he would follow
them with his binoculars. "Gooooooooaaaaaal!" shouted
Jaafar. The Sector 32 referee objected that Jaafar was sup-

porting his own team and wasn't impartial. Jaafar ignored his objections. He worried about his players as if they were his own children, and when they fell down he would check their knees and legs for any damage. Sometimes his mind would wander and for a few moments he would see them as ghosts in battle and recall the boom of artillery on the front. But then he would go back to the match and blow his whistle to award a penalty kick, as cheerful and enthusiastic as ever. He dripped with sweat as he pushed the wheelchair around with all his strength to keep up with the boys running after the ball like antelopes.

Jaafar blew the whistle. "Foul!"

"I swear it wasn't a foul, Jaafar," objected one of the boys.

"I tell you it's a foul. Don't argue, you idiot."

"But Jaafar, you were far away."

"What are these, then? Do you think I'm blind?" said Jaafar, holding up his binoculars.

The match ended in a 2-2 draw, and the boys pushed Jaafar's wheelchair to the coffee shop. He said good-bye to them and advised them to prepare for next week's match with the Sector 52 team.

Jaafar played dominoes in the Shaab coffee shop and gave the others his analysis of the quality of the various Spanish clubs. His laugh echoed through the coffee shop and shook the big picture of the imam Ali hanging on the wall. The coffee shop owner said the Americans were going to search the sector that night for weapons.

"What does that bunch of cowboys want? It's because of them I lost my legs in the Kuwait war. What do they want next? Fuck them. One day America's going to go to shit," Jaafar said indignantly, then changed the subject back to soccer. He and the Real Madrid supporters started arguing and joking. Jaafar was an avid supporter of Barcelona and sometimes Liverpool.

I was waiting for him at the coffee shop door. He came out laughing loudly and gave me a friendly punch in the guts. I pushed his wheelchair and we crossed the street. He asked after his sister, who is my wife, and I said, "She's well."

"Are you going to do the disappearing knife trick today?" he asked, coughing. He was a chronic smoker.

"No, but I may talk a little about the interpretation of dreams."

I knocked on the door and Souad opened it. "Ah, both of you," she said as she kissed Jaafar on the head. She helped me get his wheelchair through the narrow doorway. I pinched her bottom and she slapped my hand discreetly, but Jaafar didn't notice.

In the room there was a bare wooden bench, and Salih the butcher was sitting on it. Allawi was sitting cross-legged on the ground with a set of green prayer beads in his hand—the same way he sat when he was making a knife disappear.

Jaafar shook Salih's hand and said, "Hey, Allawi, come and sit on the bench."

Allawi answered proudly, "I've never sat on a chair or a bench."

"You mean in all your life?"

"Of course."

"But you're only fifteen, damn it. Anyone who heard you would say you were as old as the dinosaurs."

Jaafar laughed his booming laugh as he adjusted the photograph of his father on the wall.

Souad disappeared into the kitchen, and I sat next to the butcher. Jaafar turned his wheelchair to face us. Souad came back with a tray of tea, sat on the carpet close to Allawi, and poured the tea, smiling amiably at everyone and winking at me several times. I blew her a kiss. Jaafar turned to me and said, "Hey, lovebirds, we've got work to do. When the meeting's over you can throw each other as many kisses as you want."

In his weird woman's voice, the butcher said, "Now, Jaafar. Anyone who heard you would say this was a meeting of some underground party that was going to change the world. We've made so many knives disappear, and Souad always brings them back again. . . . And it's been going on like this for ten years."

Allawi laughed and said, "I've been making knives disappear all my life. But I want to go on making them disappear again and again, and I don't know why." Jaafar changed the subject and asked Allawi whether Umm Ibtisam would be coming today. He replied that he was certain this time, because she had sworn to him three times by Ali's son Abbas that she would come. "She must be on her way now. You know the shitty Americans have closed half the roads."

2

We were like one family. Our knife-handling skills weren't the only thing we had in common. We also shared our problems in life, our joys, and our ignorance. We were buffeted by all forms of misfortune, and several times we grew disappointed with the knives. There were other concerns in life. We almost split up on several occasions, but we were drawn back together by the strangeness and pleasure of our gift, by the feeling among all of us—except, perhaps, Salih the butcher—that knives could be a solace and give our lives the thrill of uncertainty.

Ten years have passed since we became a team in the knife trick. Allawi joined us three years ago. I continued my studies and went to the School of Education. Souad went into the sixth year of high school, specializing in the sciences, and dreamed of going to the School of Medicine. Salih the butcher has extended his shop, divorced the mother of his children, and married a young woman who had a bad reputation in the neighborhood. Jaafar found Allawi a job in the factory that makes women's shoes. He didn't want Allawi to stay in the market playing with knives. Jaafar himself was the same as always—busy with soccer, refereeing, dominoes, the coffee shop; always anxious to ensure that our group didn't fall apart and constantly seeking out new talent in soccer and also in the knife trick. He believed that our knife skills were a secret vocation that would change the world. As to how and why and when, these were all unanswered questions; he had nothing to do with them. "I've never even read a newspaper in my life. How could I understand the secret of the knives?" he said.

The butcher, Allawi, Jaafar, and I had the ability to make knives disappear. Souad was the only person who could make them reappear, but she couldn't make them disappear. Souad's difference compounded the mystery of our talents, which did not progress one step despite the passage of all those years.

Two years ago I was assigned to read books in order to find out what the knives meant, and I soon came to the idea that the knives were just a metaphor for all the terror, the killing, and the brutality in the country. It's a realistic phenomenon that is unfamiliar, an extraordinary game that has no value, because it is hemmed in by definite laws.

I married Souad a year and a half ago. It was Jaafar who arranged this early marriage with my father. Souad's cousin had approached Jaafar with a proposal to marry her. Jaafar didn't want Souad to move away from us and go to live in the village. He wasn't unaware of the tentative affection we felt for each other. My father was persuaded straightaway, especially as Jaafar made my father an attractive offer. He said he would buy Souad and me a small house. My father agreed at once because he wanted to relieve the strain in his own house. We were nine brothers and three sisters all living in two rooms, and my father was struggling to keep the family afloat. He worked as a baker and my mother gave injections to sick people in the neighborhood, though she didn't have a nursing certificate. In fact she was illiterate, and because she was so kind, people called her the angel of mercy.

When I was a youngster I played on Jaafar's soccer team. He discovered my talent by chance. He was watching me as I made a knife that some boy was holding disappear. He was ecstatic and started to hug me. He cheerfully took me to their house and introduced me to young Souad, whose eyes projected the force of life like a strong and beautiful flower. The next day Jaafar took me to Salih the butcher's shop and introduced me to him.

In those days we used to meet in Jaafar's house, but his mother and his five brothers would disturb us, so then we moved to Salih's house. He had a room on the roof of the house, where he raised birds. We would put the knives on top of a round wooden table and make them disappear one by one, then Souad would make them reappear. We would exchange views and try to analyze the trick. But the conversation soon moved away from knives and turned to jokes and stories about the people in the sector. We continued to meet in the pigeon loft until I got married and Jaafar bought us that small house. Jaafar had considerable wealth from a business he'd been in since he was young. He used to deal in pornographic magazines, which were banned, but he was careful to cover his tracks, selling them only in wealthy neighborhoods.

It was I who discovered Allawi and brought him into the group. I was in the street market buying rat poison when I saw a group of children and adults in a corner of the market, gathered in a circle, full of curiosity. Allawi was sitting cross-legged as usual, with a number of small knives of various types next to him. He didn't make knives disappear for free. People would give him a pack of cigarettes or enough money for a sandwich or to buy a grape juice or pomegranate juice, and as soon as he felt it was worth his while he would throw one of the knives onto the ground in front of the spectators and ask them to touch it to make sure it was a real knife. Then he would ask them to stand back in a slightly larger circle so that he could breathe and concentrate. Allawi stared at the knife for thirty seconds, as we all did, and as soon as tears started to glisten in his eyes the knife would disappear. The audience would applaud in amazement and admiration, and Allawi would then wait for the spectators to come up with enough money for him to repeat the trick with another knife. His main problem was that he depended on stealing knives to replace the ones he made disappear. That put him in many tricky situations.

The tears and the thirty seconds were the common denominator between us all when it came to making knives disappear and reappear. As I said, were it not for Souad, the knives would have disappeared forever and we would all have been like Allawi before he joined us—just knife thieves. Salih the butcher faced the same problem before he met Jaafar and Souad. Salih loved the trick; in his shop he would stare at knives at length until they disappeared. But after the trick he had to buy new knives. Allawi made money in the market from his gift, while Salih would lose out. If it wasn't for Souad, he said, he would have died of hunger. Every day Souad brought back the knives he had made disappear, and we were sure this was the only reason the butcher stayed with us all those years.

We were constantly on the lookout for a new member of the group, with powers like those of Souad. We would meet every Thursday and make a set of knives disappear, and Souad would make them reappear in the same way: tears and a few seconds!

I could make knives disappear easily. I began by making my mother's knives disappear in the kitchen when I was a child. In the beginning my mother would almost go crazy, but when she discovered my secret she and my father took me to a cleric to consult him on the subject. The man with the turban told them in all confidence, "Your son is in league with the jinn." He advised my father and mother to pray and wash the courtyard of the house twice—once at dawn and again at sunset. When I got interested in soccer and met Jaafar I stopped making knives disappear at home or at the homes of friends and relatives.

The knife trick didn't have a particular purpose. Maybe Salih the butcher saw his gift as a disease and as far as he was concerned Souad was the only cure. The feelings and ideas that Souad, Jaafar, Allawi, and I had were different to some extent. Jaafar thought it was a secret and sacred vocation and believed that what we did, despite the absurdity of it, was a source of great pleasure, especially as he saw himself as the spiritual father and the leader of the group.

Allawi was addicted to the game. It was like a drug that erased his memory of the painful loss of both his parents at an early age. His father had been a drunkard who argued with the neighbors and who killed a man with his pistol. Before the police arrived one of the dead man's sons, who had seen his own father drowning in blood, came to the door of Allawi's father's house with a Kalashnikov in his hand. Allawi's father was standing behind the closed door with the pistol in his hand, and his mother was trying to stop him from going out. The son emptied a whole magazine of bullets into the door. The door fell in and Allawi's mother and father were killed.

Knives were my pastime and part of my life. Seeking

the mystery of the game, I felt like someone looking for a single rare flower in a high mountain range. Often it felt like an adventure in a fable. Many a time I felt as though I was doing a spiritual exercise with the knife trick. The reality didn't interest me as much as the beauty of the mystery attracted me. Maybe this is what drove me to write poetry after I gave up looking for the meaning of the knives.

Illiteracy was one of the obstacles that compounded our failure to understand the trick or even to develop our skills throughout the years. Salih the butcher, Allawi, and Jaafar couldn't read or write. It's true that Souad was educated, but she practiced the knife trick with a childish attitude. She would always remind me, saying, "Why complicate things, my love? Life is short and we are alive. Treat the knives as a game to entertain us and leave it at that." Souad repeatedly suggested we open a little theater in the neighborhood to amuse the local people by making knives disappear and then reappear, in hopes that this might relieve the gloom of war and the endless killing. But Jaafar was worried about the clerics, because they were acting like militias at the time. I thought he was right to worry; at any moment they could have denounced us as infidels, maybe even accused us of undermining society with alien superstitions imported from abroad. Their superstitions had become the law, and God had become a sword for cutting off people's heads and declaring them infidels.

My ignorance increased when I embarked on the task of researching the knife trick through reading. My education didn't help me much. It was religious books that I first examined to find references to the trick. Most of the houses in and around our sector had a handful of books and other publications, primarily the Quran, the sayings of the Prophet, stories about heaven and hell, and texts about prophets and infidels. It's true I found many references to knives in these books, but they struck me as just laughable. They only had knives for jihad, for treachery, for torture and terror. Swords and blood. Symbols of desert battles and the battles of the future. Victory banners stamped with the name of God, and knives of war.

After that I moved into works of literature. That was by chance. A single sentence had stirred up a whirlwind of excitement inside me. Then one day, in a coffee shop, I came across an article in a local newspaper about a massacre by sectarian fighters in a village south of the capital. They had set fire to the houses of people sleeping at night. The only survivor of the conflagration was a young boy. The boy was purple, and in his hand he held a purple rat. They found him asleep in a wheat field. His story went unnoticed in the relentless daily cycle of bloody violence in the country. In the culture section of the newspaper there was an interview with an Iraqi poet in exile who said, "A closed door: That's the definition of existence."

The next day I went to Mutanabbi Street, where books are sold. I wasn't a regular visitor. I was terrified by the sight of the stacks of books there, in the bookshop windows, in the stalls in the street, and on the wooden carts. Hundreds of titles and covers. I couldn't buy a single book that day. I didn't know what to choose or where to begin. I went back to Mutanabbi Street every Friday and gradually regained my confidence. I started to buy books of poetry, novels, and short stories, local and translated. Then our group decided to contribute some money to help me buy more books, in hopes that I would come across the key to the mystery of the knives, and soon the house was full of books. We made shelves in the pigeon loft, the kitchen, and even in the bathroom. After a year of voracious reading I was no longer drawn to research into the mystery of the knives, but to the pleasures of knowledge and reading generally. The magic of words was like rain that quenched the thirst in my soul, and for me life became an idea and a dream: The idea was a ball and the dream was two tennis rackets. I didn't understand many of the books on classical philosophy. But enjoyable and interesting intellectual books on dreams, the universe, and time began to attract my attention. I felt this created a problem with the group. They would shower me with questions on what I was reading and whether I had come across any clues to the mystery of the knives in my books. I didn't know how to explain things to them. I was like a small animal that had entered the den of an enormous animal. I felt both pleasure and excitement. Perhaps I was lost, and my only compass was my passion and my fear of the diversity of life. One idea invalidated another, and one concept disguised another. One theory made another theory more mysterious. One feeling contested another. One book mocked another book. One poem overshadowed another poem. One ladder went up and another went down. Often knowledge struck me as similar to the knife trick: just a mysterious absurdity or merely a pleasant game.

I tried to explain to the group that research into knives

through books wasn't easy. It was a complicated process, and certain things might take me many more years to understand. On the other hand I didn't want to disappoint the group, especially Jaafar, who was enthusiastic about the books. So I started telling them stories about other extraordinary things that happen in this world and about man's hidden powers. I tried to simplify for them my modest knowledge of parapsychology, dreams, and the mysteries of the universe and nature. I felt that we were getting lost together, further and further, in the labyrinths of this world, without sails and without a compass.

3

Souad opened the door and a stout woman in her fifties, dressed in black, came in. She greeted us shyly. Salih the butcher made room for her on the bench and went to stand by the door. Jaafar asked him to sit down, but he said he was fine.

Souad asked the woman, Umm Ibtisam, if she would like something to drink.

"Thank you; coffee please," she said.

Jaafar tried to dispel the woman's sense that she was unwelcome. He started talking about the high price of vegetables, deploring the fact that the country was importing vegetables from neighboring countries when it had two great rivers and plenty of fertile land. Then he jumped to the subject of the high price of propane and gasoline when we had the largest reserves of black shit in the world. Souad brought Umm Ibtisam the coffee and went back to her place. She sipped the coffee and told Allawi she was in a hurry and had to get back to her children. It was Allawi who had found Umm Ibtisam. He said he was wandering around the old lanes in the center of Baghdad when he noticed a shop that sold only knives of various shapes and sizes. He went into the shop and started to browse through the knives. A woman in her fifties came up to him and offered to help. He told her he was looking for a small knife he had lost years before, with a handle in the shape of a shark. The woman gave him a puzzled look and said her knife shop was not a lost property office. Allawi preempted her, as he put it, by asking if she knew about making knives disappear. She said she didn't know what he meant and offered him a small knife with a snake wrapped around the handle. Allawi examined it and told the woman he knew how to make it disappear. He sat in the middle of the shop, and after thirty seconds of concentration and two tears, the knife disappeared. The woman was upset and asked him to leave at once.

Allawi left and went back the next day. He said he only wanted to talk to her, but she didn't want to listen. Maliciously and threateningly, Allawi told her that he could make all the knives in the shop disappear at once.

The woman pulled a large meat cleaver off one of the shelves and brandished it in Allawi's face.

"What do you want, you evil boy?" she cried.

"Nothing. Just to talk."

Allawi sat cross-legged on the floor and asked her if she would like to see another demonstration of making knives disappear. She didn't reply, just stared at him suspiciously and held the cleaver in her hand. Straight off, Allawi started telling her about the gift of making knives disappear and reappear and about our group. This was very stupid of him, because we were wary of talking about the group to outsiders, but Allawi had spent a long time in the market and thought nothing of showing off in front of others.

Allawi said, "The woman's face turned the color of tomato when I talked about the knife trick. She sat on a chair in front of me and put the cleaver on her lap. Then she started to weep in anguish." Then she suddenly stood up, closed the shop door, wiped away her tears, and told him the story of the knife shop, after making him promise never to reveal her secret.

The woman had five daughters, and her husband had been killed when a car bomb exploded in front of the Ministry of the Interior, cutting his body in half. It was a disaster. The woman had no idea how she could support her daughters. Her grief for her husband broke her heart and disrupted her sleep. She had nightmares in which she saw an enormous man slaughtering her husband with a knife. The nightmare recurred often, and every time the man would slaughter her husband with a different knife. Umm Ibtisam told Allawi she couldn't understand why the knives appeared in her dream.

A month after the nightmares started, Umm Ibtisam came across a knife in the backyard of her house. It was an old knife. She contacted her brother because she was alarmed by its sudden appearance. Her brother started to ask the neighbors about it, but they denied it was theirs. The knife aroused his interest. He said it looked like an antique. He calmed his sister down and told her he would ask his oldest son to stay a few nights with her and her daughters. The man came back a week later with a large sum of money, after selling the knife in the antique market. He told her the knife was valuable and dated from the Ottoman period. The brother joked with the woman, saying, "Let's hope you find other knives and make us really rich."

Umm Ibtisam said the nightmares then stopped. But in the same place in the yard six knives appeared, in this case kitchen knives. Umm Ibtisam kept the knives, and this time she didn't tell her brother. The knives continued to appear, and in the end she told him. He didn't tell anyone the secret of the knives, because they were waiting to see how long they would continue to appear in the yard. They kept on appearing, but it was rare for an old one to turn up. Once, a knife dating from the Abbasid period turned up; her brother sold it on the black market for a large amount. He told his sister that God was providing a livelihood for her and her daughters because her husband had been killed without good cause. He suggested opening a shop to sell the knives. The brother rented a small shop close to her house, and so Umm Ibtisam started selling knives.

Umm Ibtisam asked Jaafar to swear to keep her secret, because this was her livelihood. She added nothing to what she had told Allawi, who had invited her to attend our meeting. Jaafar swore to God and on his honor that he would keep her secret, and invited her to join the group. But she didn't take up the offer, because all she wanted was for us to leave her alone. Souad embraced

Umm Ibtisam, with tears in her eyes, perhaps for the strangeness of life's agonies.

Souad took her to the door and handed her a bag full of cake, saying, "A simple present for the girls."

None of us said anything. So there were knives appearing in other places. That meant the plot had thickened.

We were all smoking—Jaafar, Salih, Allawi, and I, and even Souad, who had slipped a cigarette out of my pack, although she didn't normally smoke. We noticed the thick cloud of smoke in the room and burst out laughing together. Jaafar began to cough like a decrepit old man. We took out our knives and started to play. I told them about the earliest book on the interpretation of dreams, which appears on a tablet from the Sumerian city of Lagash. The story goes that Gudea, the ruler of Lagash, was praying in the temple when he suddenly fell asleep.

"I'm off to work," Salih said in his effeminate voice, and left.

4

A year after I graduated from the School of Education, Jaafar the referee suddenly disappeared. We didn't leave a hospital or police station unsearched. We contacted people who had ties with some of the armed groups and kidnap gangs. But to no avail. The ground seemed to have swallowed him up, along with thousands of others in the country. Souad was in her second month of pregnancy and had postponed her studies at the School of Medicine.

I was very worried about her. She was frustrated and sad, like a bird whose wings have been broken in a storm.

The kids in Sector 29 were also sad that Jaafar had disappeared. They organized a soccer tournament by themselves for teams from the other sectors and called it the Referee Jaafar Tournament. They sent me an invitation to referee in the final.

———

The days passed slowly and sadly, like the miserable face of the country. The wars and the violence were like a photocopier churning out copies, and we all wore the same face, a face shaped by pain and torment. We fought for every morsel we ate, weighed down by the sadness and the fears generated by the unknown and the known. Our knife trick was no longer a source of pleasure, because time had dispersed those mysterious talents of ours. We had been broken one after the other, like discarded mannequins. Our group had fallen apart. There were no more meetings or discussions. Hatred had crushed our childish fingers, crushed our bones.

It wasn't easy for a recent graduate like me to find work. The religious groups had opened schools that taught children to memorize the Quran. They offered me work in their schools until I could get a government job, so I got involved in teaching children the Quran and gave up the knife business. From time to time I wrote angry, aggressive, and meaningless poems.

Allawi moved out of the capital and wandered around the towns in the south. He toured the markets showing off his skill at making knives disappear, but earned a pittance. Then we heard fresh news about him: He had broken into a restaurant and was arrested for stealing knives from the kitchen. He was sent to prison and we heard no more of him. Souad, friendly and loving, continued to visit Salih the butcher to bring his knives back, and in return Salih would give us the best cuts of meat he had.

One winter morning I was at school teaching the children the Iron Chapter of the Quran when the principal came in and told me that a strange young man wanted to talk to me about something important.

He was a tall man in his midtwenties, and his name was Hassan. He said he wanted to talk to me about Jaafar the referee. I asked the principal for permission to take a break and went to the nearby coffee shop with the man. We ordered tea and he told me what had happened to Jaafar:

The security forces had set free some hostages from a terrorist hideout; Hassan was one of the people freed. He said he had met Jaafar in the place where they were holding the hostages, a house on a farm on the outskirts of the capital. They had abducted Jaafar because he was trading in pornographic magazines in a wealthy neighborhood where policemen lived. Hassan said they had brutally tortured him. The terrorists told Jaafar that God had punished him when his legs were amputated during the war, but Jaafar hadn't repented and had gone on selling pictures of obscenities and debauchery. So the terrorists had decided to cut off Jaafar's arms as a lesson to any unbelieving profligate. The terrorists assembled all the hostages to witness the process of amputating Jaafar's arms. They couldn't believe what happened next. Hassan said that whenever the terrorists approached Jaafar, the swords they were holding disappeared, and tears were streaming from his eyes. The terrorists didn't have a single sword or knife left. They were terrified of Jaafar and said he was a devil. They stripped him naked in front of us and crucified him against the wall. They hammered nails into the palms of his hands, and he started writhing in pain, naked, with no legs. They decided to amputate his arms with bullets. Two men stood in front of him and sprayed bullets into his arms. One of the bullets hit his heart, and he died instantly. They dragged his body to the river, collected some dry branches, and poured some gas on him. They set fire to him and chanted, "God is most great."

Souad and I had a beautiful boy, and we called him Jaafar. I continued working in the religious school. I never managed to tell Souad what had happened to her brother. I suppressed the horror that his death caused, and I loved Souad even more. She was my only hope in life. She went back to the School of Medicine, and time began to heal the wounds, slowly and cautiously.

Umm Ibtisam came to see us. Her financial situation had greatly improved. She said we were good people and she hadn't forgotten us. She offered to open a large shop in the neighborhood for us to sell knives.

Our business was profitable, though sometimes I would unwittingly make one knife or another disappear. At night I would start by kissing Souad's toes, then creep up to her thighs, then to her navel, her breasts, her armpits and neck, until I reached her ear, and then I would whisper, "My love, I need help!"

She would pinch me on the bottom, then climb on top of my chest, strangle me with her hands, and say, "Ha, you wretch, how many knives have you made disappear? I'm not going to get them back until you kiss me a thousand and one times."

I kissed every pore on her body with passion and reverence, as if she were a life that would soon disappear.

When young Jaafar was five years old, his gift emerged: Like his mother, he could make knives reappear.

The Composer

JAAFAR AL-MUTALLIBI WAS BORN IN THE TOWN OF al-Amara. In 1973 he resigned from the Communist party and joined the ruling Baath party. In the same year his wife gave birth to their second son. Jaafar was a professional lute player and a renowned composer of patriotic songs. He was killed in the uprising in the city of Kirkuk in 1991.

———

Today I can tell you about how he died. Do you see this old woman shouting out the price of fish? She's my mother. We've been selling fish since we came back to Baghdad. Let me help her empty the crate of fish, then let's go to a nearby coffee shop and talk.

———

After the end of the war between Iraq and Iran my father started to proclaim his atheism blatantly and caused us many problems. One evening he came home with his shirt stained with blood. It seems he'd had a nosebleed after one of his friends punched him. They were playing dominoes in the coffee shop when my father launched into a tirade of obscene insults to God and the Prophet. He made

them up and set them to music during the game. As you
know, he was a well-known composer. At first my father
whistled a tune composed in the military style, then he
added a new insult: a nail in the testicle of your imam's
sister.

Many people burst out laughing when they heard the
insults my father's imagination came up with, but they
soon began to keep away from him and ask God for for-
giveness. Some of them avoided meeting him in the street.
One of them told him in jest one day that he hoped a truck
loaded with steel would run him over, but everyone was
frightened of his connection with the government. The
day after he was punched he wrote a report for party
headquarters about Abu Alaa, the man who hit him, and
two days later Abu Alaa disappeared. We were living in a
neighborhood called the Second Qadissiya, which con-
sisted of houses the government had assigned to junior
army officers, other people who had moved from cities in
the south and center of the country, and the families of
Kurds who worked for the regime. We were the only family in the neighborhood that earned its living differently.
All the families except ours lived off salaries from the army,
the party, and the security services, while we lived off the
patriotic songs that my father composed. My father had a
status higher than that of the mayor and members of the
local hierarchy of the party, because the President himself
had more than once awarded him military medals for his
songs about the war, songs people remember to this day.

Listen, brother, I'll sum up the story for you. One year
after the war ended, my father suffered what the newspapers call writer's block, and he was unable to compose

new music for the many poems celebrating the greatness
of the President that famous poets would send him.
Months passed, then a year, and he still could not write a
single new tune. Do you know what he did in the meantime? He took it upon himself to write and set to music
short depraved poems making fun of religion. One warm
winter evening we were watching television when we
heard my father singing a new song of his about the Prophet's wives and how loose they were. Suddenly my elder
brother sprang up, took my father's pistol from the wardrobe, jumped on top of my father, and put the pistol in his
mouth. He would have killed him were it not for my
mother, who tore open her dress, baring her breasts and
screaming. My brother was transfixed for a moment as he
looked at my mother's enormous breasts, which hung
down over her stomach like an animal whose guts had
spilled out. This was the first time we had ever seen my
mother's breasts, except as babies. I went into the bathroom, and my brother fled the sight of my mother by leaving the house. She was illiterate, but she was smarter than
my father, whom she looked after in a curious way. She
spoiled him as if he were a son. She was the licensed mid-
wife in the Qadissiya district, and people were very fond of
her. My father decided to submit a report on my brother to
the local party headquarters, but they did not react to it.

My father's name had started to stink in the neighborhood and in artistic circles. They said that Jaafar al-
Mutallibi had gone mad, and his old friends avoided him.
He traveled to Baghdad and submitted a request to the
radio and television station asking them to rebroadcast
the war songs he had composed, or at least one song a

week. They rejected his request and told him his songs were now inappropriate. They were only broadcasting patriotic songs twice a year: on the anniversary of the outbreak of the war and the anniversary of when it had ended. My father wanted to restore his past and his fame by any means possible. He tried but failed to meet the President. He submitted an application to the film and theater department, proposing a documentary film about his songs and his music, but that request was also ignored.

While he was making all these attempts he finished composing the music to ten songs insulting God and existence, as well as a beautiful song about the first four caliphs. We realized he had gone completely mad when he started frequenting the studios and trying to persuade them to record him singing his songs making fun of religion. Of course, his requests were rejected categorically, and some people threw him out and threatened to kill him. In the end my father decided to record his songs on tape at home. He sat in front of a tape recorder and started to sing and play the lute. Of course, it was a poor recording, but it was intelligible. He played it to us at breakfast; we were worried that people would find out about this tape. We tried to get hold of it and destroy it, but he would never let it leave his coat pocket, and when he went to sleep he would slip it into a special pocket he had made in the pillow.

Today there's no need to hide this copy, because others need it, and religion has made more progress than necessary, along with the murderers and thieves. The reaction of the street might be hysterical, but let's fire a bullet in the air. Go ahead, you're a journalist; it will be good for you and good for everyone. A young singer offered to sing it and record it again in a modern studio, but I refused. These songs must remain as my father himself recorded them, as evidence of his story. They can only be copied. People soon forget the stories of this event. When you tell them these stories, after a time they think the stories are figments of imagination. Take our neighbor in the market, for example: Abu Sadiq, who sells onions. When he now tells his story about the battle with the Iranians at the river Jassim, it sounds like a Hollywood horror story he made up.

The government army ran away, and the Kurdish Peshmerga militias entered Kirkuk. The people of the city welcomed the uprising with great joy. There was overwhelming chaos, gunfire, dead bodies, Kurdish dancing, and songs everywhere. We were unable to escape. The insurgents set fire to houses in all the government districts and where party members lived. They killed and strung up the bodies of the Baathists, police, and security people.

We were holed up at home, and a group of young men broke down the reinforced door to my father's office. They took us out on the street to carry out the death sentence on us. My mother was on her knees pleading with them, but she did not rip her clothes this time. What? My father? No, no, my father wasn't with us. Months before the uprising, he had become the madman of the city, wandering the streets singing against God and carrying his lute, which no longer had a single string. A fire broke out in our house, and my mother collapsed unconscious as the rest of us leaned against the outer wall of the house. Umm Tariq, our Kurdish neighbor, turned up at the last moment, screaming at the young men and speaking to them in their language. Then she started imploring them to set us free. She told them how kind and generous my mother was and how she helped the Kurdish women give birth and looked after pregnant women. She told them how my mother would give away bread to the neighbors in honor of Abbas, the son of the Imam Ali, at feast time, and how brave my elder brother was and how he'd been best friends with her son who'd been killed fighting with the Peshmerga forces during the Anfal campaign, and that it was he who helped her late son escape from Kirkuk (here she lied), and that I was a good, peaceful boy who wouldn't hurt a fly. She ended her defense of us on an angry note. "They're not responsible for what that pimp Jaafar al-Mutallibi has been doing," she said. Then she spat on the ground. We went into Umm Tariq's house and we didn't leave until the Republican Guard forces entered the city and the Peshmerga militias withdrew. Most of the insurgents ran away with the militias.

In the end we found my father without a head, tied to a farm tractor with a thick rope. He had been dragged around the city streets for a whole day, and his corpse had been put on display in a manner that is impossible to imagine. At the time they were about to execute us my father was close to the local party headquarters, where the bodies of the party members filled the courtyard. My father went into the empty building and headed for the information room. He knew this room well because it was from this room that his patriotic songs used to be broadcast from loudspeakers on the roof during the first war.

From the same loudspeakers the party members would also speak to the public when someone was being executed for deserting the army or for helping the Peshmerga militias. My father put the tape into the tape player and the loudspeakers started broadcasting to the insurgents his songs attacking God and existence. My father was hugging his lute and smiling when the insurgents arrived. They took him outside—

Excuse me, my friend. There's a fish dealer who's bringing some sacks of carp, so I have to go now. Tomorrow I'll tell you the secret of my father's relationship with Umm Tariq, the Kurdish woman.

The Song of the Goats

PEOPLE WERE WAITING IN LINES TO TELL THEIR stories. The police intervened to marshal the crowd, and the main street opposite the radio station was closed to traffic. Pickpockets and itinerant cigarette vendors circulated among them. People were terrified a terrorist would infiltrate the crowd and turn all these stories into a pulp of flesh and fire.

Memory Radio had been set up after the fall of the dictator. From the start, the radio station had adopted a documentary approach to programming, without news bulletins or songs, just documentary reports and programs that delved into the country's past. The station had become famous after announcing that it was going to record a new program titled *Their Stories in Their Own Voices*. Crowds gathered at the broadcasting center from across the country. The idea was simple: to select the best stories and record them as narrated by the people involved, but without mentioning their real names; then the listeners would choose the top three stories, which would win valuable prizes.

I succeeded in filling out the application form but

made it inside the radio station only with great difficulty. More than once an argument broke out because of the crush. Old and young, adolescents, civil servants, students, and unemployed people all came to tell their stories. We waited in the rain for more than four hours. Some of us were subdued; others were bragging about their stories. I saw one man with no arms and a beard that almost reached his waist. He was deep in thought, like a decrepit Greek statue. I noticed the anxiety of the handsome young man who was with him. From a Communist who was tortured in the seventies in the Baath party's prisons, I heard that the man with the beard had a story that was tipped to win, but that he himself had not come to win. He was just a madman, but his companion, one of his relatives, coveted the prize. The man with the beard was a teacher who went to the police one day to report on a neighbor who was trading in antiquities stolen from the National Museum. The police thanked him for his cooperation. The teacher, his conscience relieved, went back to his school. The police submitted a report to the Ministry of Defense that the teacher's house was an al Qaeda hideout. The police were in partnership with the antiquities smuggler. The Ministry of Defense sent the report to the U.S. Army, who bombed the teacher's house by helicopter. His wife, his four children, and his elderly mother were killed. The teacher escaped with his life, but he suffered brain damage and lost his arms.

I personally had more than twenty stories teeming in my memory about my long years of captivity in Iran. I was confident that at least one of them would really be the clincher in the competition.

They took in the first batch of contestants and then announced to the crowds left behind us that they had stopped accepting applications for the day. There were more than seventy of us who went in. They had us sit down in a large hall similar to a university cafeteria. A man in a smart suit then told us we were first going to listen to two stories to understand the format of the program. He also spoke about legal aspects of the contracts we would have to sign with the radio station.

The lights gradually dimmed and the hall fell silent, as if it were a cinema. Most of the contestants lit up cigarettes, and we were soon enveloped in a thick cloud of smoke. We started listening to a story by a young woman, whose voice reached us clearly from the four corners of the hall. She told how her husband, a policeman, had been held by an Islamist group for a long time and how, during the sectarian killings, the killers had sent his body back decomposed and decapitated. When the lights came back on, chaos broke out. Everyone was talking at the same time, like a swarm of wasps. Many of them ridiculed the woman's story and claimed they had stories that were stranger, crueler, and more crazy. I caught sight of an old woman close to ninety waving her hand in derision and muttering, "That's a story? If I told my story to a rock, it would break its heart."

The man in the smart suit came back on and urged the contestants to calm down. In simple words he explained that the best stories did not mean the most frightening or the saddest; what mattered was authenticity and the style of narration. He said the stories should not necessarily be about war and killing. I was upset by what he said, and I noticed that most of the contestants paid no attention. A man the size of an elephant whispered in my ear, "It's bullshit what that bullshitter says. A story's a story, whether it's beautiful or bullshit."

The lights went down again and we started listening to the second story.

———

"They found her feeding me shit. A whole week she was mixing it with the rice, the mashed potatoes, and the soup. I was a sallow child, three years old. My father threatened to divorce her, but she took no notice. Her heart was hardened forever. She never forgave me for what I did, and I will never forget how cruel she was. By the time she died of cancer of the womb, the storms of life had carried me far away. I escaped from the country sometime after the barrel incident, abject, defeated, paralyzed by fear. On the night I said good-bye to my father, he walked with me to the graveyard. We read the first chapter of the Quran over my uncle's grave. We embraced and he slipped a bundle of cash into my hand. I kissed his hand and disappeared.

"We were living in a poor part of Kirkuk. The neighborhood didn't have mains drainage. People would have septic tanks dug in their yards for ten dollars. Nozad the Kurdish vegetable seller was the only person in the neighborhood who specialized in digging those tanks. When Nozad died his son Mustafa took on the work. They found Nozad burned to a cinder in his shop after a fire broke out one night. No one knows what Nozad was doing that night. Some people claim he was smoking hashish. My father didn't believe that. For all kinds of disasters his favorite proverb was 'Everything we do in this ephemeral world is written, preordained.' So in my childhood I believed that 'our life' was tucked away somewhere in schoolbooks or in the shop where they sold newspapers. My father wanted to save my childhood with all the good-will and love he possessed. He was gracious toward others and toward life in a way that still puzzles me today. He was like a saint in a human slaughterhouse. Disaster would strike us pretty much every other year. But my father didn't want to believe that fate could bring such a mysterious curse. Perhaps he attributed it to destiny. We were vulnerable to assault from every direction—from the unknown, from reality, from God, from people, and even the dead would come back to torment us. My father tried to bury my crime through various means, or at least erase it from my mother's memory. But he failed. In the end he gave in. He left the task to the ravages of time, in hopes that this would efface the disaster.

"I may have been the youngest murderer in the world: a murderer who remembered nothing of his crime. For me, at least, it was no more than a story, just a story to entertain people at any moment. What I noticed was that everyone would write, intone, or sing the story of my crime as they fancied. At the time, my father wasn't working in the pickle business. He was a tank driver, and the war was in its first year. My mother was nagging my father for a third child, but he refused because of the war, which terrified him. We were comfortably off. Every month my father would send enough money to cover food, clothing, and the rent on the house. My mother would spend her time either asleep or visiting my aunt, with whom she'd talk all day about the price of fabric and the waywardness of men.

"In the summer, my mother would go off into a dream world. She wouldn't listen, or talk, or even look. The midday heat would wipe her out. At noon she would take a bath and then sleep naked in her room like a dead houri.* When night fell she would recover some of her vitality, as if she had come out of a coma. She would watch her favorite soap opera and news programs in which the President awarded medals for bravery to heroic soldiers, thinking that my father might appear among them.

"At noon one day, my mother dozed off with her arms and legs splayed open under the ceiling fan. My brother and I—he was a year younger—slipped off into the courtyard. There was nothing out there but a solitary fig tree and the cover of the septic tank. I remember my mother used to cry under the fig tree whenever one of our relatives died or some disaster struck us. The mouth of the tank was covered with an old kitchen tray held down by a large stone. We, my brother and I, had trouble moving the stone. Then we started throwing pebbles into the tank. It was our favorite game. Umm Alaa, our neighbor, used to make us paper boats, which we would sail on the surface of the pool of shit.

"They say I pushed my brother into the tank and ran off to the roof of the house to hide in the chicken coop. When I grew up, I asked them, 'Might he have fallen in, and I run away out of fear?' They said, 'You confessed yourself.' Perhaps they questioned me like the dictator's

---

* Houri: one of the beautiful virgins of the Quranic paradise.

police. I don't remember anything. But they would tell their stories about it as if they were describing the plot of a film they'd enjoyed. All the neighbors took part in the rescue attempt. They couldn't find the truck that used to come once a month to empty out the septic tanks in the neighborhood. They used everything they could find to get the shit out of the tank: pots and pans, a large bucket, and other vessels. It was an arduous and disgusting task, like torture in slow motion. It was the height of summer, and the foul odors added to the horror and the shock. Before the sun went down, they brought him out—a dead child shrouded in shit.

"My father was late coming back from the front. My uncle wrote him a letter and then took care of arrangements for the burial of my brother. We buried him in the children's cemetery on the hill. It may have been the most beautiful cemetery in the world. In the spring, wildflowers of every color and variety would grow there. From a distance, the graveyard looked like the crown of an enormous, colored tree: a cemetery whose powerful fragrance spread for miles around. A week later our neighbor Umm Alaa opened the door and saw my mother. The intensity of the grief had driven her to distraction. She had put shit in a small bowl, and was mixing it into my food very slowly with a plastic spoon, then filling my mouth with it as she wept.

"My father sent me to live with my uncle, and I became a refugee of sorts. I would visit our house as a guest every Friday, escorted by my aunt, who kept an eye on my mother. I felt like a ball that people kicked around. That's how I spent six years, trying to understand what was happening around me. I had to learn what their feelings and their words meant, all the while wearing a chain of thorns around my neck. It was like crawling across a bed of nails. The septic tank was the bane of my childhood. On more than one occasion I heard how life apparently advances, moves on, sets sail, or, at worst, crawls slowly forward. My life, on the other hand, simply exploded like a firecracker in the sky of God, a small flare in his mighty firmament of bombardment. I spent the remaining years of my childhood and adolescence watching everyone carefully, like a sniper hidden in the darkness. Watching and shooting. Against the horrors of my life I unleashed other nightmares, imaginary ones. I invented mental images of my mother and others being tortured, and in my schoolbook I drew pictures of enormous trucks crushing the heads of children. I still remember the picture of the President printed on the cover of our workbooks. He was in military uniform, smiling, and under his picture were written the words, 'The pen can shoot bullets as deadly as the rifle.'

"There was a cart that brought kerosene, drawn by a donkey. It came through the lanes in the neighborhood in winter. The children would follow behind, waiting for the donkey's awesome penis to grow erect. I used to shut my eyes and imagine the donkey's penis, gross and black, going into my mother's right ear and coming out of the left. She would scream for help because of the pain.

"A year before the war ended my father lost his left leg and his testicles. This forced my mother to take me back. My father decided to go back to the trade practiced by his father and his forefathers: making pickles. They say my grandfather was the most famous pickle seller in the city of Najaf. The King himself visited him three times. I went back home and acted as my father's drudge and obedient servant. I was happy, because my father was a miracle of goodness. Despite everything he had suffered in his life he remained faithful to his inner self, which had somehow not been warped by the pain. He had an artificial leg fitted, and his capacity for love seemed to grow. He pampered my mother and showered her with gifts—gold necklaces, rings, and lingerie embroidered with flowers.

"My father tiled the courtyard and made a concrete cover for the septic tank. He left some space for the fig tree, but it died from the brine he used in the pickles. My mother wept beneath it for the last time when I was sixteen. The government in Baghdad had built a road for the highway and removed the old cemetery. Her father's grave had been there. For a long time we were sad about the loss of my grandfather's bones.

"The courtyard was full of plastic barrels for pickling; piles of sacks full of cucumbers, eggplants, green and red peppers, cabbages, and cauliflowers; bags of salt, sugar, and spices; bottles of vinegar; and tins of molasses. There were also large cooking pots, which were always full of boiling water, to which we would add spices, then all the vegetables one by one. My father wasn't as proficient as his father, let alone his grandfather. He started trying out new methods. He had spent a large part of his life in tanks and had forgotten many of the family recipes for making pickles. The tank had cost him his balls, his leg, *and* the trade of his forefathers.

"I would sit opposite my mother for hours, cutting up

eggplants or stuffing cucumbers with garlic or celery. Her tongue was as poisonous as a viper. The summer no longer bothered her. She had turned into a fat cow, burned by the sun, with a loose tongue, and she smoked to excess. Noxious weeds had sprouted in her heart. People took pity on her, with words as poisonous as hers. 'Poor woman,' they said. 'An impotent husband and no children, just the bird of ill omen.' The bird—that was me, and I showed all the signs of ill omen. My father was busy all the time with the accounts and dealing with the shops in the market and moving barrels in the old pickup. After sunset he would collapse from fatigue. He would have dinner, pray, and tell us about his pickle problems, then take off his artificial leg and go to bed to tickle his gray-haired wife with his fingers.

"When the war over Kuwait broke out, I was meant to join the army. My father and my uncle sat down to discuss the question of my military service. My uncle had never seen the horrors of the front in the Iran War. He was working in the security department in the city center. My father made up his mind: He would not give me up to die. 'How can I let them kill my only son?' My uncle argued with him, trying to explain how it would affect him in his branch of security if his nephew avoided serving the flag ('Do you want them to execute us all—us *and* the women?'). My father stuck to his position. My uncle threatened to arrest me in person if I didn't join the army, but my father threw him out of the house. 'Listen,' he said, 'it's true I'm a peaceful man, but this is my son, a piece of my flesh. If you persist in this, I'll slit your throat.' My uncle had been drunk that night and raging like a bull. He left shouting further insults. My father stood up, performed his prayers, and quickly calmed down. 'God save me from the accursed devil,' he said. 'He's my brother. It was just drunken talk. I know him. He has a good heart.'

"I was a prisoner in the house for three months. The streets were full of military police and all the security agencies. My father decided I shouldn't work by day in case the neighbors noticed me. At night I would slip out into the yard like a thief, with a lantern in my hand. I would sit next to the sacks of eggplants, cucumbers, and peppers, busy with my work and thinking about my life. I would mix arak with water in an empty milk can so as not to get caught by my father, then get drunk and snack on the many varieties of pickle this tank driver had to offer. The alcohol would flow in my blood, and I would crawl like a baby toward the septic tank, press my ear against the concrete cover, and listen. I could hear him laughing. I would shut my eyes and imagine the feel of his bare shoulder. His skin was hot from all the playing and exertion. I no longer remembered his face. My mother had the only photograph of him, and she wouldn't let anyone else go near it. She hid it in the wardrobe. She put the picture in a small wooden box decorated with a peacock.

"At the crack of dawn my father would get up. He would usually find me asleep in my place. He would put his hand on my forehead and I would wake up to his touch. 'Go inside, son. Perform your prayers. May God prosper you.' He was well aware I was drinking arak, but religion to him didn't mean the words of any prophet, any holy law or prohibitions. Religion meant love of virtue, as he would put it to anyone with whom he was discussing questions of Islamic law.

"I will never forget the day he broke down in tears at the soccer field. He frightened the children, and I was embarrassed and disturbed that he was crying. The Baath party members had executed three young Kurds close to the soccer field. They tied them to wooden stakes and shot them dead in full view of the local people. Before they did it, they announced over loudspeakers, 'These people are traitors and terrorists who do not deserve to eat from the bounty of this land or drink its water or breathe its air.' As usual, the Baathists took the bodies and left the stakes in place to remind everyone of what had happened. My father had come to the square to take me to the cinema. He was crazy about Indian films. When he saw that one goal was missing an upright he realized we had taken the stakes to make the goals. Traces of blood had dried on the wood. My father broke down when one of the children said, 'We're still missing one goalpost. Maybe they'll execute another one and we can have the stake.'

"One summer evening we were invaded again. My uncle knocked frantically on the door. My mother was counting money and putting it in an empty tomato paste jar. My father and I were playing chess. He could beat me easily, but first he enjoyed giving me the pleasure of taking his pawns. He would sacrifice them and his other pieces without taking anything in return, keeping only his king and queen. Then he would start to destroy my pieces with his black queen until he had me in checkmate.

"My father went out to the yard to greet my uncle. My

mother threw on her shawl and followed. They all stood near the septic tank in anxious discussion, but in low voices. I watched them from behind the windowpane. I was still dizzy from drinking the day before. I was waiting for night to come to get drunk again. My mother rushed to fetch something from under the stairs. My father and my uncle worked together to empty a barrel full of pickled cauliflower. My mother came back with a hammer and a nail. My father laid the barrel flat on the ground and started to punch holes in it at random with the nail. He didn't have his artificial leg on. He was hopping around the barrel on one leg as if he were playing or dancing. My uncle parked the pickup outside the front door and loaded it with the barrels of pickles. Then my father came into the living room sweating.

"'Listen, son,' he said, 'there's no time. Your uncle has information that the police and the party are going to search all the houses at dawn. Your uncle has loyal friends in the village of Awran. Stay there a few days till things calm down.' I climbed into the empty barrel and my mother closed the lid tight. My father and my uncle lifted me onto the pickup.

"My father was right. They were brothers, after all, and they could read each other's minds. My uncle drove through the streets like a madman to save my life. He managed to reach the outskirts of the city safely, but all the roads to the provincial towns and villages had military checkpoints. His only option was to take the back roads. He chose a road through the wheat fields to the east of the city. Maybe in his panic he mistook the road. Even the city children knew the chain of rugged and rocky hills that lay beyond the wheat fields. Maybe images of the people tortured in his department had unhinged his brain. Maybe he imagined his colleagues dissolving him in tanks of sulphuric acid and the headline SECURITY OFFICER HELPS NEPHEW ESCAPE IN PICKLE BARREL. As he drove through the wheat fields, he was barely in control of the steering wheel. The bumps were about to break my ribs, and only dust kicked up by the truck crept in through the holes in the barrel. The barrel stank like the dead cats on the neighborhood trash heap. Did my uncle pull out fingernails, gouge out people's eyes, and singe their skin with branding irons in the vaults of the security department? Maybe it was the souls of his victims that drove him into the ravine, maybe it was my own evil soul, or maybe it was the soul that preordained everything that is ephemeral and mysterious in this transitory world.

"Seven barrels lay in the darkness at the bottom of the cliff like sleeping animals. The pickup had overturned after my uncle tried to take a second rocky bend in the hill. The barrels rolled down into the ravine with the truck. I spent the night unconscious inside the barrel. In the first hours of morning the rays of sunlight pierced the holes in the barrel, like lifelines extended to a drowning man. My mouth was full of blood and my hands were trembling. I was in pain and frightened. I started to observe the rays of the sun as they crisscrossed confusingly in the barrel. I wanted to escape the chaos that had played havoc with my consciousness. I felt as if I had smoked a ton of marijuana: a fish coming to its senses in a sardine tin, a dead worm in an abandoned well, a putrid fetus with crushed bones in a womb the shape of a barrel. Then my mind fixed on another image: my brother sinking to the bottom of the septic tank and me diving after him.

"The bleating sounded faint at first, as though a choir was practicing. One goat started and then another joined in, then all the goats together, as if they had found the right key. The rays of the sun moved and fell right in my eye. I pissed in my pants inside that barrel, appalled at the cruelty of the world to which I was returning. The goatherd called out to his flock, and one of the goats butted the barrel."

The Reality and the Record

EVERYONE STAYING AT THE REFUGEE RECEPTION *center has two stories—the real one and the one for the record. The stories for the record are the ones the new refugees tell to obtain the right to humanitarian asylum, written down in the immigration department and preserved in their private files. The real stories remain locked in the hearts of the refugees, for them to mull over in complete secrecy. That's not to say it's easy to tell the two stories apart. They merge and it becomes impossible to distinguish between them. Two days ago a new Iraqi refugee arrived in Malmö, in southern Sweden. He was in his late thirties. They took him to the reception center and did some medical tests on him. Then they gave him a room, a bed, a towel, a bedsheet, a bar of soap, a knife, fork, and spoon, and a cooking pot. Today the man is sitting in front of the immigration officer telling his story at amazing speed, while the immigration officer asks him to slow down as much as possible.*

———

They told me they had sold me to another group; they were very cheerful. They stayed up all night drinking whiskey and laughing. They even invited me to join them in a drink, but I declined and told them I was a religious man. They bought me new clothes, and that night they cooked me a chicken and served me fruit and sweets. It seems I fetched a good price. The leader of the group even shed real tears when he said good-bye. He embraced me like a brother.

"You're a very good man. I wish you all the best, and good luck in your life," said the man with one eye.

I think I stayed with the first group just three months. They had kidnapped me on that cold accursed night. That was in the early winter of 2006. We had orders to go to the Tigris; it was the first time we had received instructions directly from the head of the emergency department in the hospital. At the bank of the river the policemen were standing around six headless bodies. The heads had been put in an empty flour sack in front of the bodies. The police guessed they were the bodies of some clerics. We had arrived late because of the heavy rain. The police piled the bodies onto the ambulance driven by my colleague Abu Salim, and I carried the sack of heads to my ambulance. The streets were empty; the only sounds to break the forlorn silence of the Baghdad night were some gunshots in the distance and the noise of an American helicopter patrolling over the Green Zone. We set off along Abu Nawas Street toward Rashid Street, driving at medium speed because of the rain. I remembered the words the director of the emergency department in the hospital often used to say: "When you're carrying an injured person or a patient close to death, the speed of the ambulance shows how humane and responsible you are.

But when you are carrying severed heads in an ambulance, you needn't go faster than a hearse drawn by mules in a dark medieval forest."

The director saw himself as a philosopher and an artist, but "born in the wrong country," as he would say. He took his work seriously nonetheless and considered it a sacred duty, because to him running the ambulance section of the emergency department meant managing the dividing line between life and death. We called him the Professor; my other colleagues hated him and called him mad. I know why they hated him, because the enigmatic and aggressive way he spoke made him seem screwed up in the eyes of others. But I retained much respect and affection for him because of the beautiful and fascinating things he said. Once he said to me, "Spilled blood and superstition are the basis of the world. Man is not the only creature who kills for bread, or love, or power, because animals in the jungle do that in various ways, but he is the only creature who kills because of faith." He would usually wrap up his speeches by pointing to the sky and declaiming theatrically, "The question of humanity can be solved only by constant dread." My colleague Abu Salim had a notion that the Professor had links with the terrorist groups because of the violent language he used, but I would loyally defend the man, because they did not understand that he was a philosopher who refused to make foolish jokes, as the stupid ambulance drivers did all day. I remembered every sentence and every word he said, for I was captivated by my affection and admiration for him.

Let me get back to that wretched night. When we

turned toward the Martyrs Bridge I noticed that the
ambulance driven by Abu Salim had disappeared. Then in
the side mirror I caught sight of a police car gaining on us
at high speed. I pulled over to the side in the middle of the
bridge. Four young men in masks and special police uni-
forms got out of the police car. The leader of the group
pointed his pistol in my face and told me to get out of the
vehicle, while his colleagues unloaded the sack of heads
from the ambulance.

"I've been kidnapped and they are going to cut off my
head." That was my first thought when they tied me up
and stuffed me in the trunk of the police car. It took me
only ten minutes to realize what was awaiting me. I
recited the Throne Verse from the Quran three times in
the darkness of the trunk, and I felt that my skin was
starting to peel off. For some reason in those dark
moments I thought about my body weight, maybe 155
pounds. The slower the car went, or the more it turned,
the more frightened I was, and when it picked up speed
again a strange blend of tranquility and anxiety would
pulse through me. Perhaps I thought at those moments of
what the Professor had said about the correlation between
speed and the imminence of death. I didn't understand
exactly what he meant, but he would say that someone
about to die in the forest would be more afraid than someone about to die in a speeding ambulance, because the
first one feels that fate has singled him out, while the second imagines there are others sticking with him. I also
remember that he once announced with a smile, "I would
like to have my death in a spaceship traveling at the speed
of light."

I imagined that all the unidentified and mutilated bodies I had carried in the ambulance since the fall of Baghdad lay before me, and that in the darkness surrounding me I then saw the Professor picking my severed head from a pile of trash, while my colleagues made dirty jokes about my liking for the Professor. I don't think the police car drove very far before it came to a halt. At least they did not leave the city. I tried to remember the Rahman Verse of the Quran, but they got me out of the car and escorted me into a house that smelled of grilled fish. I could hear a child crying. They undid my blindfold, and I found myself in a cold, unfurnished room. Then three madmen laid into me and beat me to a pulp, until a darkness again descended.

I thought I heard a cock crow at first. I shut my eyes, but I couldn't sleep. I felt a sharp pain in my left ear. With difficulty I turned over onto my back and pushed myself toward the window, which had recently been blocked up. I was very thirsty. It was easy to work out that I was in a house in one of Baghdad's old neighborhoods. That was clear from the build of the room and particularly the old wooden door.

In fact I don't know exactly what details of my story matter to you for me to get the right of asylum in your country. I find it very hard to describe those days of terror, but I want to mention also some of the things that matter to me. I felt that God, and behind him the Professor, would never abandon me throughout my ordeal. I felt the presence of God intensely in my heart, nurturing my peace of mind and calling me to patience. The Professor kept my mind busy and alleviated the loneliness of my captivity. He was my solace and my comfort.

Throughout those arduous months I would recall what the Professor had said about his friend, Dawoud the engineer. What did he mean by saying that the world is all interconnected? And where do the power and the will of God stand in such matters? We were drinking tea at the hospital door when the Professor said, "While my friend Dawoud was driving the family car through the streets of Baghdad, an Iraqi poet in London was writing a fiery article in praise of the resistance, with a bottle of whiskey on the table in front of him to help harden his heart. Because the world is all interconnected, through feelings, words, nightmares, and other secret channels, out of the poet's article jumped three masked men. They stopped the family car and killed Dawoud, his wife, his child, and his father. His mother was waiting for them at home. Dawoud's mother doesn't know the Iraqi poet nor the masked men. She knows how to cook the fish that was awaiting them. The Iraqi poet fell asleep on the sofa in London in a drunken stupor, while Dawoud's mother's fish went cold and the sun set in Baghdad."

The wooden door of the room opened and a young man, tall with a pale and haggard face, came in carrying breakfast. He smiled at me as he put the food down in front of me. At first I was uncertain what I could say or do. But then I threw myself at his feet and implored him tearfully, "I am the father of three children. . . . I'm a religious man who fears God. . . . I have nothing to do with politics or religious denominations. . . . God protect you . . . I'm just an ambulance driver . . . before the invasion, and since the invasion. . . . I swear by God and his noble Prophet." The young man put a finger to his lips and rushed out. I felt that my end had come. I drank the cup of tea and performed my prayers in hopes that God would forgive my sins. At the second prostration I felt that a layer of ice was forming across my body and I almost cried out in fear, but the young man opened the door, carrying a small lighting device attached to a stand, and accompanied by a boy carrying a Kalashnikov rifle. The boy stood next to me, pointing the gun at my head, and from then on he did not leave his place. A fat man in his forties came in, taking no notice of me. On the wall he hung a black cloth banner inscribed with a Quranic verse urging Muslims to fight jihad. Then a masked man came in with a video camera and a small computer. Then a boy came in with a small wooden table. The masked man joked with the boy, tweaked his nose, and thanked him, then put the computer on the table and busied himself with setting up the camera in front of the black banner. The thin young man tried out the lighting system three times and then left.

"Abu Jihad, Abu Jihad!" the fat man shouted.

The young man's voice came from outside the room: "Wait a minute. Right you are, Abu Arkan."

This time the young man came back carrying the sack of heads they had taken from the ambulance. Everyone blocked their nose because of the stink from the sack. The fat man asked me to sit in front of the black banner. I felt that my legs were paralyzed, but the fat man pulled me roughly by my shirt collar. At that point another man came in, thick-set with one eye, and ordered the fat man to let me be. This man had in his hand an army uniform. The man with one eye sat close to me, with his arm across

my shoulders like a friend, and asked me to calm down.
He told me they wouldn't slaughter me if I was coopera-
tive and kindhearted. I didn't understand fully what he
meant by this "kindhearted." He told me it would only
take a few minutes. The one-eyed man took a small piece
of paper from his pocket and asked me to read it. Meanwhile the fat man was taking the decomposing heads out
of the sack and lining them up in front of me. It said on the
piece of paper that I was an officer in the Iraqi army and
these were the heads of other officers, and that accompanied by my fellow officers I had raided houses, raped women,
and tortured innocent civilians; that we had received
orders to kill from a senior officer in the U.S. Army, in
return for large financial rewards. The man with one eye
asked me to put on the army uniform, and the cameraman
asked everyone to pull back behind the camera. Then he
came up to me and started adjusting my head, as a hair-
dresser does. After that he adjusted the line of heads, then
went back behind the camera and called out, "Off you go."

The cameraman's voice was very familiar. Perhaps it
resembled the voice of a famous actor, or it might have
been like the voice of the Professor when he was making
an exaggerated effort to talk softly. After they filmed the
videotape, I didn't meet the members of the group again,
other than the young man who brought me food, and he
prevented me from asking any questions. Every time he
brought food he would tell me a new joke about politicians and men of religion. My only wish was that he
would let me contact my wife, because I had hidden some
money for a rainy day in a place where even the jinn would
never think of looking, but they vehemently rejected my

request. The one-eyed leader of the group told me that everything depended on the success of the videotape, and in fact the tape was such a success so quickly that everyone was surprised. Al Jazeera broadcast the videotape. They allowed me to watch television, and on that day they were jumping for joy, so much so that the fat man kissed me on the head and said I was a great actor. What made me angry was the Al Jazeera news anchor, who assured viewers that the channel had established through reliable sources that the tape was authentic and that the Ministry of Defense had admitted that the officers had gone missing. After the success of the broadcast they started treating me in a manner that was better than good. They took trouble over my food and bedding and allowed me to take a bath. Their kindness culminated on the night they sold me to the second group. Then three masked men from that group came into the room, and after the man with one eye had given me a warm farewell, the new men laid into me with their fists, tied me up and gagged me, then shoved me into the trunk of a car that drove off at a terrifying speed.

The second group's car traveled far this time. Perhaps we reached the outskirts of Baghdad. They took me out in a desolate village where dogs roamed and barked all over the place. They held me in a cattle pen; there were two men who took turns guarding the pen night and day. I don't know why, but they proceeded to starve me and humiliate me. They were completely different from the first group. They wore their masks all the time and never spoke a word with me. They would communicate with each other through gestures. In fact there was not a human voice to be heard from the village, just the barking of dogs the whole month I spent in the cow pen.

The hours passed with oppressive tedium. I would hope that anything would happen, rather than this life sentence with three cows. I gave up thinking about these people, or what religious group or party they belonged to. I no longer bemoaned my fate but felt I had already lived through what happened to me at some time, and that time was a period that would not last long. But my sense of this time made it seem slow and confused. It no longer occurred to me to try to escape or to ask them what they wanted from me. I felt that I was carrying out some mission, a binding duty that I had to perform until my last breath. Perhaps there was a secret power working in league with a human power to play a secret game for purposes too grand for a simple man like me to grasp. "Every man has both a poetic obligation and a human obligation," as the Professor used to say. But if that was true, how could I tell the difference, and easily, between the limits of the human obligation and those of the poetic obligation? Because my understanding is that, for example, looking after my wife and children is one of my human obligations, and refusing to hate is a poetic obligation. But why did the Professor say that we confuse the two obligations and do not recognize the diabolical element that drives them both? Because the diabolical obligations imply the capacity to stand in the face of a man when he is pushing his own humanity toward the abyss, and this is too much for the mind of a simple man like me, who barely completed his intermediate education, at least I think so.

What I'm saying has nothing to do with my asylum request. What matters to you is the horror. If the Professor were here, he would say that the horror lies in the simplest of puzzles that shine in a cold star in the sky over this city. In the end they came into the cow pen after midnight one night. One of the masked men spread one corner of the pen with fine carpets. Then his companion hung a black banner inscribed, "The Islamic Jihad Group, Iraq Branch." Then the cameraman came in with his camera, and it struck me that he was the same cameraman as the one with the first group. His hand gestures were the same as those of the first cameraman. The only difference was that he was now communicating with the others through gestures alone. They asked me to put on a white dishdasha and sit in front of the black banner. They gave me a piece of paper and told me to read out loud what was written on it: that I belonged to the Mehdi Army and I was a famous killer, I had cut off the heads of hundreds of Sunni men, and I had support from Iran. Before I'd finished reading, one of the cows gave a loud moo, so the cameraman asked me to read it again. One of the men took the three cows away so that we could finish off the cow pen scene.

I later realized that everyone who bought me was moving me across the same bridge. I don't know why. One group would take me across the Martyrs Bridge toward Karkh on the west bank of the Tigris, then the next group would take me back across the same bridge to Rasafa on the east bank. If I go on like this, I think my story will never end, and I'm worried you'll say what others have said about it. So I think it would be best if I summarize the story for you, rather than have you accuse me of making it up.

They sold me to a third group. The car sped across the Martyrs Bridge once again. I was moved to a luxurious house, and this time my prison was a bedroom with a lovely comfortable bed, the kind in which you see film stars having sex. My fear evaporated and I began to grasp the concept of the secret mission for which they had chosen me. I carried out the mission so as not to lose my head, but I also thought I would test their reaction in certain matters. After filming a new video in which I spoke about how I belonged to Sunni Islamist groups and about my work blowing up Shiite mosques and public markets, I asked them for some money as payment for making the tape. Their decisive response was a beating I will never forget.

Throughout the year and a half of my kidnapping experience, I was moved from one hiding place to another. They shot video of me talking about how I was a treacherous Kurd, an infidel Christian, a Saudi terrorist, a Syrian Baathist intelligence agent, or a Revolutionary Guard from Zoroastrian Iran. On these videotapes I murdered, raped, started fires, planted bombs, and carried out crimes that no sane person would even imagine. All these tapes were broadcast on satellite channels around the world. Experts, journalists, and politicians sat there discussing what I said and did. The only bad luck we ran into was when we made a video in which I appeared as a Spanish soldier, with a resistance fighter holding a knife to my neck, demanding Spanish forces withdraw from Iraq. All the satellite stations refused to broadcast the tape because Spanish forces had left the country a year earlier. I almost paid a heavy price for this mistake, when the group holding me wanted to kill me in revenge for what had happened, but the cameraman saved me by suggesting another wonderful idea, the last of my videotape roles. They dressed me in the costume of an Afghan fighter, trimmed my beard, and put a black turban on my head. Five men stood behind me, and they brought in six men screaming and crying out for help from God, his Prophet, and the Prophet's family. They slaughtered the men in front of me like sheep as I announced that I was the new leader of the al Qaeda organization in Mesopotamia and made threats against everyone in creation.

Late one night the cameraman brought me my old clothes and took me to the ambulance, which was standing at the door. They put those six heads in a sack and threw it into the vehicle. At that moment I noticed the cameraman's gestures, and I thought that surely he was the cameraman for all the groups and maybe the mastermind of this dreadful game. I sat behind the steering wheel with trembling hands. Then the cameraman gave the order from behind his mask: "You know the way. Cross the Martyrs Bridge, to the hospital."

I am asking for asylum in your country because of everyone. They are all killers and schemers—my wife, my children, my neighbors, my colleagues, God, his Prophet, the government, the newspapers, even the Professor who I thought an angel, and now I have suspicions that the cameraman with the terrorist groups was the Professor himself. His enigmatic language was merely proof of his connivance and his vile nature. They all told me I hadn't been away for a year and half, because I came back the morning after working that rainy night, and on that very morning the Professor said to me, "The world is just a bloody and hypothetical story, and we are all killers and heroes." And those six heads cannot be proof of what I'm saying, just as they are not proof that the night will not spread across the sky.

———

Three days after this story was filed away in the records of the immigration department, they took the man who told it to the psychiatric hospital. Before the doctor could start asking him about his childhood memories, the ambulance driver summed up his real story in four words: "I want to sleep."

    It was a humble entreaty.

That Inauspicious Smile

THE SAYING "THE BODY MUST BE PROTECTED, NOT the thoughts"* sprang to his mind as he sat on the toilet seat in a Chinese restaurant. He speculated that his mind wanted to solve the puzzle of "Why that damned smile when I wake up in the morning?" He came out of the restroom and asked for a cup of green tea. He had left the house early that day, before his wife and daughter had gotten up. From the restaurant he sent his wife a text message saying he had gone out for a short walk and would be back in an hour. Now the hour was running out. He remembered that yesterday she had asked him to buy a new vacuum cleaner on Monday. Just then he noticed two old women sitting in a corner of the restaurant, doing a crossword in the newspaper together. One of them was holding the pen and the other was thinking, with a finger on her nose. The day before, the vacuum cleaner had stopped working when he was cleaning the little girl's room. Now he saw the reflection of his smile in the teacup, and it turned green.

---

* Attributed to Albert Camus.

He began to think about the question of thoughts and the body as he watched the two women. Before going into the restaurant he'd witnessed a group of children standing at the traffic lights waiting for green. They stood in two lines with two teachers, one at the front and one at the back. He guessed how many children there were—twelve, of the future hope variety. His mind wagged its tail with delight. They would no doubt be doctors, engineers, murderers, poets, alcoholics, and unemployed people, twelve children being the new cover of an old story. His mind slowly moved forward, and he began to smell the stench of death. Those are our children and the ones who will visit our graves, he said. Twelve ideas crossing the street, cheerful and energetic. They are the powerhouse of the future.

He stood up and headed to the bathroom again. He washed his face for the tenth time, but the smile was still stuck there. If he had not had trouble with fantasies in the past, he would have behaved like any sensible man, looked in the mirror, and said, "Impossible." But he was used to surprises, and his experiences had taught him not to waste time looking for reasons for his predicaments and to look for the emergency exit instead. His mind guessed that the smile had come to him from a previous dream. It was a naive, cinematic dream that had absolutely nothing to do with his past:

He kisses her on the lips and tries to climb the stairs, then sits back down at the foot of them. He smiles and leans his head against the wall. She brushes her teeth in the kitchen and shouts out to him, asking him to bring the bedsheet. She wants to wash it. But now he's going down a well like a feather tumbling through the air. He is far from the light, a dead man who doesn't hear her last call. Four years after this stair incident the woman dies. They find her lying on the kitchen table with the toothbrush in her hand and, on the brush, a piece of meat the size of an ant.

Shall we say that after the woman brushes her teeth, the rays of the sun stream through the window, or that the rain is beating the windowpane? The dream recurs every night. There's a need for this ancient music, and yet how many of these timeless death stories have disappeared? What eternal naïveté there is in tales about our beautiful death! These little stories that are pointed like a toothbrush. Why did we contrive to complicate these death stories? A giant shadow poses these questions to the man in the dream.

In the morning the man woke up smiling, then he saw his smile in the mirror. It seemed to have stayed stuck there after the dream. Once, in an unusual discussion with a member of the Association for the Defense of the Luckless, he said:

"I didn't want my wife and daughter to see me smiling like an idiot for no reason. It was an insignificant smile. It was wide, but it didn't show my damaged teeth. My lips were sealed like the lips of a clown. I rubbed my face with soap and water, but the smile was still stuck there. I brushed my teeth three times, but it stayed there like indelible ink. I thought, 'Maybe it will disappear as the day proceeds, as the snow melts on a sunny morning.' I don't know how such thoughts occurred to me. Then suddenly I felt intensely hot, although the season was winter. I put on a light sports shirt printed on the back with a picture of a black crow standing on a basketball. The ball was marked like a map of the world. I put on a clean pair of jeans and my black winter coat. I resolved to solve the mystery of that smile. The wife and daughter have put up with much—I worry I might drive them mad—because I've had a succession of disasters in this world. I'm not luckless, so stop sticking that stupid label on me.

"The snow was dancing down. It was amazing and beautiful. For the first time the sky was so munificent, when it yielded all these jewels to me. I had known feelings like these before. You wake up and smell a morning, then you think, 'Life still suits me.' There are disguised moments of sadness that hide in various clothes and smells. You get drunk and weep and think you have cleared away a large rock blocking the channels of your day, which had come to an end with a painful blow. A man I don't know passed close by me, wearing a heavy winter coat, a woolen scarf wrapped around his neck, and on his head a black hat, on which the snowflakes had gathered. He kept looking and turning toward me with a smile as he walked in the opposite direction. I wanted to return his smile. I passed my fingers along my lips. So I didn't need a new smile. I made do with turning toward him quickly to offer him in return that dream smile of mine.

"I went into the Chinese restaurant to have some tea and check up on the smile in the mirror. I saw two old lesbians doing the crossword puzzle. I sent my wife a second message on my phone, telling her I would be back a little late and would go straight to the shops to buy the vacuum cleaner. I had to find a solution for the damned smile. I thought of going to the hospital. Perhaps I'm ill and the smile is just an alarm bell. But instead of that I found myself going into a cinema and buying a ticket. I felt a nasty fever spreading through my body. There were some girls under a large poster of next week's film. What stood out was Dracula's fangs and the blood running down from the corners of his mouth. There was a smile on the face of this monster. The girls sat down as though they were in class at school. All of them gave me stiff looks, with a tinge of fear. Then they smiled in turn, from right to left. I was sitting in front of them. I took off my coat and turned my back on them so that they could clearly see the basketball and the crow. Don't ask me why I did that. Do you have an answer to this damned smile? Then I checked on the features of my face in the mirrors in the foyer. I confess I was somewhat satisfied with this new smile. At least I don't have to contract my face muscles in order to smile, as other people do. I forgot to tell you that one of the old lesbians told me to keep this beautiful smile because the Finns are gloomy in winter and look depressed, which makes the winter darker and more dreary.

"The film was a disgusting, fast-paced tearjerker. The heroine set fire to her house with her husband and children inside. Now she's screaming and sobbing in front of the fire and the neighbors have their fingers on their mouths as though they are about to vomit. The elegant lady sitting near me was drowning in tears. She turned slowly toward me and muttered in shock, 'The pig!' I turned to her in disbelief. Then she looked at me again but this time disdainfully. She began to look back and forth like an imbecile between the disaster of the heroine in the film and my beaming face. She looked as though she were revolted and wanted to slap me because of my smile. I wanted to explain to her, 'I'm not smiling at what happened to the woman and her house, lady (although she's a bitch like you). I woke up this morning and found this smile had been forced upon me.'

"I ignored the woman and tried to pretend I pitied the woman in the film, who took a revolver out of her belt and fired a bullet into her head amid a crowd of people, who quickly dispersed when the fire engines arrived.

"When the lights came on in the cinema, the elegant lady stood up and insulted me, this time out loud. 'Animal, son of a bitch!' she shouted.

"The audience turned toward me, but all they did was smile as they looked at my face. Were they smiling at the insult, or at the crow on the ball, or because I answered the woman's insult with my cold smile? I have to get rid of this smile as soon as possible. My wife called me; I lied and said I was still looking for a suitable vacuum cleaner.

"The snow kept falling, and it sparkled even more when a light wind rose and made it fall at a slant. I was frightened and confused, thinking that this smile might appear when some disaster happens. What if a bus runs over someone now and his guts come out of his ass? Surely there would be a panicky crowd. What if they noticed my smile as I joined them in watching this free spectacle? Without doubt they would give me a thorough beating. How would I explain to them that my smile had nothing to do with what had happened? Or who would put up with you smiling in his face when, for example, his baby was dying of hunger in front of his eyes? Could you calmly explain to him that you are smiling in derision at life, which produced this child without reason and then took it away with a kick in the guts, also without reason? Wouldn't the father and mother of this child stab you and tear apart this hard-hearted animal? I hurried off to a bar nearby. The body must be protected, not the thoughts. What if you were to lose control over the inherited communal gestures that unite us in fear and in happiness?

"I felt a stomach pain when I went into the bar, which was suspiciously crowded. The Finns start drinking early in the day. My arrival in the bar set off a smile-fest, but the smiles gradually waned and turned into laughs and intermittent comments that were, technically, quick insults. At first I didn't understand why the bartender hesitated when I ordered a beer. Then he said, 'You should drink up your beer quickly and leave.' In turn I looked at the other customers, angry at such an unfriendly reception. What kind of bar is this? I said that out loud, but as you know, I was smiling in spite of myself. Perhaps they had the notion that I was just a tame animal that had taken more than his fair share. There were four young men with shaved heads in black leather jackets. Only then did I realize that this was a neo-Nazi bar. They were making fun of my daring or my stupidity, looking at me between one drink and another and making ugly jokes and insults. Then one of them stood up, took out his cock, and waved it in my face. Everyone burst out laughing, including the bartender. I thought I would keep myself under control, drink the beer quickly, and escape this filthy trap. But I was stupid. I pretended to be brave and indifferent. I sat there like a captain smiling on his ship. But the bartender, that son of a whore, asked me to leave at once, for fear of problems. Of course, I was delighted with this expulsion. And so I left the Nazis' bar like a frightened mouse.

"It was Sunday and I had thought it was Monday. At least I remembered that, and then I thought my wife would be angry when she read my text messages. Which electrical goods stores are these that open on Sunday? Now, what other lie could I make up to cover my first lie? I thought of going home and confessing everything to my wife. The smile would be proof I was telling the truth. But my feelings were contradictory. Then I entered a small shop, bought six bottles of beer, and went to the park. Do I really have bad luck? Or was I born by mistake?

"The streets were empty, and the wind was playing havoc and making a racket when it tried to shift things from their place. The wind blew over a price list parked outside a closed restaurant, then it brought along a large cardboard box, which flew around like half of a dismembered body. There were empty cigarette packs racing each other about. Unconsciously I hummed a tune. I wanted to sing, but I did not know which song to choose. I didn't have the words to any song in my head. A slight anxiety came over me. Had the words to songs been sucked out of my memory to this extent? All I could do was make up some little songs. I kept humming in hopes that I would come across some words in a while, but stupid tears came instead of words. The wind blew an empty white bag, which passed close to my ear and made me forget the tune. It had frightened me. The bag did a somersault at the junction as though it was deciding which way to go. It rose uncertainly for a moment, then fell in a lurch to the asphalt. This time the wind dragged it along the ground in spite of itself and left it next to the trash that had accumulated at the mouth of the street drain.

"I reached the yard thinking about how I had lied to my wife. Definitely she would be convinced I'd had a date with a woman. Now she would be in a rage, stuffing my clothes into a suitcase in readiness to throw me out.

"When I looked through the thick trees I thought at first that the wind had blown in some other black bags, but in reality it had brought those four young men with shaved heads. With the instinct of an animal I sensed danger. I caught their smell when they came close to me. For no reason I stood up to piss behind a giant tree. Two of them surrounded me on the right and the others on the left. They looked like Guardian Angels. They took out their cocks and all of them pissed with vigor, like donkeys that had not pissed for years. As they pissed they looked at me stiffly and contemptuously because of my cock, which out of fear had not released a single drop. I was easy prey, and cowardly. The noise of their piss gushing out filled the air, like a waterfall cascading in the darkness. The wind died down, or slowed down to make space for the symphony of their pissing. The smell of it drifted up to my brain like poisonous nerve gas, or perhaps the wind wanted to give the sky a free look.

"Everything was over with lightning speed. In just a few minutes they gave vent to all possible animal instincts, giving me a thorough beating. Then they ran off, as though the wind had picked them up, hidden them in the folds of its solemn cloak, and gone back to work after the youths had carried out their mission to perfection. I was bleeding from my ear, my nose, my teeth, and my eye, and from the blocked nostrils of my soul as well. I tried to get up. I wished that this wind, a slave to the sky in blind obedience and allegiance, would pick me up too, but it didn't. It was sweeping up everything but my empty body, which lay bleeding by the tree, as though what had happened was part of a humorous story full of banal scrapes. I saw empty bags of every color and shape. They were hovering around me at crazy speeds, as though they were making me a special offer of leftover bones, times, and places. They did not seem happy with me, nor did the force blowing them. A torn gray bag flew past, and I realized it was my mother's shawl. A burned brain flew by on giant wings. A shoal of fish swam past, carrying scraps of a young girl's flesh. The flying vipers of economic sanctions flew by, wrapped around their food of humans and dreams. All my wife's underwear went past, one pair dripping blood, another semen, the next one ink, and so on. My old notebooks passed by, clapping their covers. Scorpions in a bottle went past, my summer shirts, medicines that had expired, and cartons of baby milk. Bread went by on wings of shit. Poems passed, pissing on themselves like disabled children. With their savage dogs the guards on the borders I had walked across went past. My cross-eyed brother, who wears the turban of an imam. My severed and bloodied fingers flew by, my daughter, Mariam, in her pram, disfigured because I loved her too much. My wife went by, playing a trumpet that screeched like an owl.

"My whole life passed page by page, all the jams and scrapes I had been through, page after page. Even when I closed my eyes it didn't stop. Pain and vertigo had me in their power. The pages went past in the darkness, white page after page."

———

In the evening the man was laid out on a bed in the hospital, smiling at his wife and his daughter, who was holding a beautiful bunch of flowers.

"Why are you smiling like that, Daddy?" Mariam asked in surprise.

The Nightmares of Carlos Fuentes

IN IRAQ HIS NAME WAS SALIM ABDUL HUSAIN, AND he worked for the municipality in the cleaning department, part of a group assigned by the manager to clear up in the aftermath of explosions. He died in Holland in 2009 under another name: Carlos Fuentes.

Bored and disgusted as on every miserable day, Salim and his colleagues were sweeping a street market after an oil tanker had exploded nearby, incinerating chickens, fruit and vegetables, and some people. They were sweeping the market slowly and cautiously for fear they might sweep up with the debris any human body parts left over. But they were always looking for an intact wallet or perhaps a gold chain, a ring, or a watch that could still tell the time. Salim was not as lucky as his colleagues in finding the valuables left over from death. He needed money to buy a visa to go to Holland and escape this hell of fire and death. His only lucky find was a man's finger with a valuable silver ring of great beauty. Salim put his foot over the finger, bent down carefully, and with disgust pulled the silver ring off. He picked up the finger and put it in a black bag where they collected all the body parts. The ring ended up on Salim's finger; he would contemplate the gemstone in surprise and wonder, and in the end he abandoned the idea of selling it. Might one say that he felt a secret spiritual relationship with the ring?

When he applied for asylum in Holland he also applied to change his name: from Salim Abdul Husain to Carlos Fuentes. He explained his request to the official in the immigration department on the grounds that he was frightened of the fanatical Islamist groups, because his request for asylum was based on his work as a translator for the U.S. forces, and his fear that someone might assassinate him as a traitor to his country. Salim had consulted his cousin who lived in France about changing his name. He called him on his cell phone from the immigration department because Salim had no clear idea of a new foreign name that would suit him. In his apartment in France his cousin was taking a deep drag on a joint when Salim called. Suppressing a laugh, his cousin said, "You're quite right. It's a hundred times better to be from Senegal or China than it is to have an Arab name in Europe. But you couldn't possibly have a name like Jack or Stephen—I mean, a European name. Perhaps you should choose a brown name—a Cuban or Argentine name would suit your complexion, which is the color of burnt barley bread." His cousin was looking through a pile of newspapers in the kitchen as he continued the conversation on the phone, and he remembered that two days earlier he had read a name, perhaps a Spanish name, in a literary article of which he did not understand much. Salim thanked his cousin warmly for the help he had given him and wished him a happy life in the great country of France.

Carlos Fuentes was very happy with his new name, and the beauty of Amsterdam made him happy too. Fuentes wasted no time. He joined classes to learn Dutch and promised himself he would not speak Arabic from then on, or mix with Arabs or Iraqis, whatever happened in life. "Had enough of misery, backwardness, death, shit, piss, and camels," he said to himself. In the first year of his new life Fuentes let nothing pass without comparing it with the state of affairs in his original country, sometimes in the form of a question, sometimes as an exclamation. He would walk down the street muttering to himself sulkily and enviously, "Look how clean the streets are! Look at the toilet seat; it's sparkling clean! Why can't we eat like them? We gobble down our food as though it's about to disappear. If this girl wearing a short skirt and showing her legs were now walking across Eastern Gate Square, she would disappear in an instant. She would only have to walk ten yards and the ground would swallow her up. Why are the trees so green and beautiful, as though they're washed with water every day? Why can't we be peaceful like them? We live in houses like pigsties while their houses are warm, safe, and colorful. Why do they respect dogs as much as humans? Why do we masturbate twenty-four hours a day? How can we get a decent government like theirs?" Everything Carlos Fuentes saw amazed him and humiliated him at the same time, from the softness of the toilet paper in Holland to the parliament building protected only by security cameras.

Carlos Fuentes's life went on as he had planned it. Every day he made progress in burying his identity and his past. He always scoffed at the immigrants and other foreigners who did not respect the rules of Dutch life and who complained all the time. He called them "retarded gerbils." They work in restaurants illegally, they don't pay taxes, and they don't respect any law. They are Stone Age savages. They hate the Dutch, who have fed and housed them. He felt he was the only one who deserved to be adopted by this compassionate and tolerant country, and that the Dutch government should expel all those who did not learn the language properly and anyone who committed the slightest misdemeanor, even crossing the street in violation of the safety code. Let them go shit there in their shitty countries.

After learning Dutch in record time, to the surprise of everyone who knew him, Carlos Fuentes worked nonstop, paid his taxes, and refused to live on welfare. The highlight of his efforts to integrate his mind and spirit into Dutch society came when he acquired a good-hearted Dutch girlfriend who loved and respected him. She weighed two hundred pounds and had childlike features, like a cartoon character. Fuentes tried hard to treat her as a sensitive and liberated man would, like a Western man, in fact a little more so. Of course, he always introduced himself as someone of Mexican origin whose father had left his country and settled in Iraq to work as an engineer with the oil companies. Carlos liked to describe the Iraqi people as an uncivilized and backward people who did not know what humanity means. "They are just savage clans," he would say.

Because of his marriage to a Dutch woman, his proficiency in Dutch, his enrollment in numerous courses on Dutch culture and history, and the fact that he had no legal problems or criminal record in his file, he was able to obtain Dutch citizenship sooner than other immigrants could even dream of, and Carlos Fuentes decided to celebrate every year the anniversary of the day he became a Dutch national. Fuentes felt that his skin and blood had changed forever and that his lungs were now breathing real life. To strengthen his determination he would always repeat, "Yes, give me a country that treats me with respect, so that I can worship it all my life and pray for it."

That's how things were until the dream problem began and everything fell to pieces, or as they say: Proverbs and old adages do not wear out; it's only man that wears out. The wind did not blow fair for Fuentes. The first of the dreams was grim and distressing. In the dream he was unable to speak Dutch. He was standing in front of his Dutch boss and speaking to him in an Iraqi dialect, which caused him great concern and a horrible pain in his head. He would wake up soaked in sweat, then burst into tears. At first he thought they were just fleeting dreams that would inevitably pass. But the dreams continued to assail him without mercy. In his dreams he saw a group of children in the poor district where he was born, running after him and making fun of his new name. They were shouting after him and clapping: "Carlos the coward, Carlos the sissy, Carlos the silly billy." These irritating dreams evolved night after night into terrifying nightmares. One night he dreamt that he had planted a car bomb in the center of Amsterdam. He was standing in the courtroom, ashamed and embarrassed. The judges were strict and would not let him speak Dutch, with the intent to humiliate and degrade him. They fetched him an Iraqi translator, who asked him not to speak in his incomprehensible rustic accent, which added to his agony and distress.

Fuentes began to sit in the library for hours looking through books about dreams. On his first visit he came across a book called *The Forgotten Language*, by Erich Fromm. He did not understand much of it, and he did not like the opinions of the writer, which he could not fully grasp because he had not even graduated from middle school. "This is pure bullshit," Fuentes said as he read Fromm's book: "We are free when we are asleep, in fact freer than we are when awake. . . . We may resemble angels in that we are not subject to the laws of reality. During sleep the realm of necessity recedes and gives way to the realm of freedom. The existence of the ego becomes the only reference point for thoughts and feelings."

Feeling a headache, Fuentes put the book back. How can we be free when we cannot control our dreams? What nonsense! Fuentes asked the librarian if there were any simple books on dreams. The librarian did not understand his question properly, or else she wanted to show off how cultured and well read she was on the subject. She told him of a book about the connection between dreams and food and how one sleeps, then she started to give him more information and advice. She also directed him to a library that had specialist magazines on the mysteries of the world of dreams.

Fuentes's wife had noticed her husband's strange behavior, as well as the changes in his eating and sleeping habits and in when he went into and came out of the bathroom. Fuentes no longer, for example, ate sweet potato, having previously liked it in all its forms. He was always buying poultry, which was usually expensive. Of course, his wife did not know he had read that eating any root vegetable would probably be the cause of dreams related to a person's past and roots. Eating the roots of plants has an effect different from that of eating fish, which live in water, or eating the fruits of trees. Fuentes would sit at the table chewing each piece of food like a camel, because he had read that chewing it well helps to get rid of nightmares. He had read nothing about poultry, for example, but he just guessed that eating the fowl of the air might bring about dreams that were happier and more liberated.

In all his attempts to better integrate his dreams with his new life, he would veer between what he imagined and the information he found in books. In the end he came to this idea: His ambition went beyond getting rid of troublesome dreams; he had to control the dreams, to modify them, purge them of all their foul air, and integrate them with the salubrious rules of life in Holland. The dreams must learn the new language of the country so that they could incorporate new images and ideas. All the old gloomy and miserable faces had to go. So Fuentes read more and more books and magazines about the mysteries of sleep and dreams according to a variety of approaches and philosophies. He also gave up sleeping naked and touching his wife's naked skin. In bed he began to wear a thick woolen overcoat, which gave rise to arguments with his wife, and so he had to go to the sitting room and sleep on the sofa. Nakedness attracts the sleeper to the zone of childhood; that's what he read too. Every day at 12:05 exactly he would go and take a bath, and after coming out of the bathroom he would sit at the kitchen table and take some drops of jasmine oil. Before going to bed at night he would write down on a piece of paper the main sedative foods, which he would buy the following day. This state of affairs went on for more than a month, and Fuentes did not achieve good results. But he was patient and his will was invincible. As the days passed he started to perform mysterious secret rituals: He would dye his hair and his toenails green and sleep on his stomach repeating obscure words. One night he painted his face like an American Indian, slept wearing diaphanous orange pajamas, and put under his pillow three feathers taken from various birds.

Fuentes's dignity did not permit him to tell his wife what was happening to him. He believed it was his problem and he could overcome it, since in the past he had survived the most trying and miserable conditions. In return his wife was more indulgent of his eccentric behavior, because she had not forgotten how kind and generous he was. She decided to give him another chance before intervening and putting an end to what was happening.

On one beautiful summer night Carlos Fuentes was sleeping in a military uniform with a toy plastic rifle by his side. As soon as he began to dream, a wish he had long awaited came true for the first time: He realized in his dream that he was dreaming. This was exactly what he had been seeking, to activate his conscious mind inside the dream so that he could sweep out all the rubbish of the unconscious. In the dream he was standing in front of the door to an old building that looked as though it had been ravaged by fire in its previous life. The building was in central Baghdad. What annoyed him was seeing things through the telescopic sights of the rifle he was holding in his hands. Fuentes broke through the door of the building and went into one flat after another, mercilessly wiping out everyone inside. Even the children did not survive the bursts of bullets. There was screaming, panic, and chaos. But Fuentes had strong nerves and picked off his victims with skill and precision. He was worried he might wake up before he had completed his mission, and he thought, "If I had some hand grenades I could very soon finish the job in this building and move on to somewhere else." But on the sixth floor a surprise hit him when he stormed the first apartment and found himself face-to-face with Salim Abdul Husain! Salim was standing naked next to the window, holding a broom stained with blood. With a trembling hand Fuentes aimed his rifle at Salim's head. Salim began to smile and repeated in derision, "Salim the Dutchman, Salim the Mexican, Salim the Iraqi, Salim the Frenchman, Salim the Indian, Salim the Pakistani, Salim the Nigerian . . ."

Fuentes's nerves snapped and he panicked. He let out a resounding scream and started to spray Salim Abdul Husain with bullets, but Salim jumped out the window and not a single bullet hit him.

When Fuentes's wife woke up to the scream and stuck her head out the window, Carlos Fuentes was dead on the pavement, and a pool of blood was spreading slowly under his head. Perhaps Fuentes would have forgiven the Dutch newspapers, which wrote that an Iraqi man had committed suicide at night by jumping from a sixth-floor window, instead of writing that a Dutch national had committed suicide. But he will never forgive his brothers, who had his body taken back to Iraq and buried in the cemetery in Najaf. The most beautiful part of the Carlos Fuentes story, however, is the image captured by an amateur photographer who lived close to the scene of the incident. The young man took the picture from a low angle. The police had covered the body; the only part that protruded from under the blue sheet was his outstretched right hand. The picture was in black and white, but the stone in the ring on Carlos Fuentes's finger glowed red in the foreground, like a sun in hell.